"Please, would you give me a drink of water?"

It was then that the man spoke to her. With a start, she straightened and glanced around.

He sat leaning against the trunk of a small tree growing near the well, with his back to her. She wondered how he knew she was there.

His hair was brown, the color of almonds that had been roasted . . . his shoulders, broad and muscular, filled out the tunic seam to seam in such obvious strength that she was reminded of the gladiators she'd seen as a child in Sebaste.

"Please, would you give me a drink of water?" he asked.

She realized there was a presence about him that was causing her to stare at him very impolitely . . .

Biblical Fiction by Gloria Howe Bremkamp
From Here's Life Publishers

Mara, The Woman at the Well
The Woman Called Magdalene (July '91)
Phoebe, A Leader Before Her Time
    (March '92)

MARA

THE WOMAN AT THE WELL

GLORIA HOWE BREMKAMP

Here's Life Publishers

First Printing, February 1991

Published by
HERE'S LIFE PUBLISHERS, INC.
P. O. Box 1576
San Bernardino, CA 92402

Library of Congress Cataloging-in-Publication Data
Bremkamp, Gloria Howe.
    Mara : the woman at the well / Gloria Howe Bremkamp.
        p.   cm.
    ISBN 0-89840-304-9
    1. Samaritan woman (Biblical character) — Fiction.
2. Bible. N.T. — History of Biblical events — Fiction. I. Title.
PS3552.R369M34   1990
813'.54 — dc20   90-21959
                                                CIP

Cover design and illustration by Ami Blackshear

For More Information, Write:
L.I.F.E. — P.O. Box A399, Sydney South 2000, Australia
Campus Crusade for Christ of Canada — Box 300, Vancouver, B.C., V6C 2X3, Canada
Campus Crusade for Christ — Pearl Assurance House, 4 Temple Row, Birmingham, B2 5HG, England
Lay Institute for Evangelism — P.O. Box 8786, Auckland 3, New Zealand
Campus Crusade for Christ — P.O. Box 240, Raffles City Post Office, Singapore 9117
Great Commission Movement of Nigeria — P.O. Box 500, Jos, Plateau State Nigeria, West Africa
Campus Crusade for Christ International — Arrowhead Springs, San Bernardino, CA 92414, U.S.A.

For a special person in my life,

SUZANNE,

my niece.

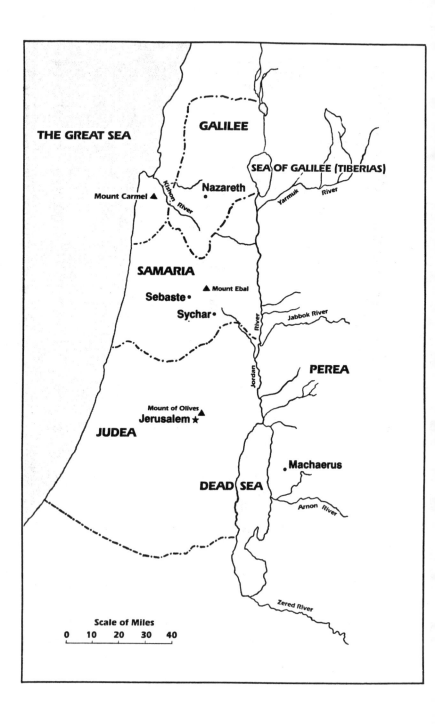

THE GREAT SEA

GALILEE

SEA OF GALILEE (TIBERIAS)

Mount Carmel ▲

Kishon River

● Nazareth

Yarmuk River

SAMARIA

▲ Mount Ebal

Sebaste ●

Sychar ●

Jabbok River

Jordan River

PEREA

Mount of Olives ▲

Jerusalem ★

JUDEA

Machaerus ●

DEAD SEA

Arnon River

Zered River

Scale of Miles

0   10   20   30   40

Why did she stay with him?
Was no man to ever really love her,
or be gentle with her, or care for her?

1

MARA RAN BLINDLY, tears spilling onto her face.

She'd been no match for Coniah's brute strength. The more she had struggled against him, the harder he had hit her. Only when she went limp against him had he loosened his hold on her.

It was then she had started running, dodging between the squalid houses of her neighbors, scurrying up narrow alleys, shoving her way through throngs of people in the street that led up the hill toward the palace . . . and beyond to safety.

There were many hiding places in the city of Sebaste. She had sought out all of them at one time or another during the years she had been married to Coniah. But the safest one for her on this day was located in a grove of trees growing outside the palace wall at the far side of the royal hill.

She reached the top of the hill, stopped and looked back. Her breath came hard and fast, in a race with the pounding of her heart. Below, she saw Coniah still searching for her amid the clutter of squalid houses.

Fresh panic pushed at her. She fled again toward the place of safety atop the hill where the great palace, built for Caesar Augustus, was situated.

At the point where the wall of the palace angled sharply, the trail narrowed. She slowed her dash of panic, forced herself to pick a cautious way along the rocky overgrowth. To her left, the hill dropped off almost vertically. At the bottom, she could see the towering stone columns that flanked the length of the Via Augustan and the shops lining both sides of it. On the sloping hills across the valley stretched the olive orchards owned by the Tetrarch Herod Antipas, and in which her father and her brother-in-law worked as gardeners.

On any other day, she would have relished the sight of the distant olive orchards in an imaginary pretense of power over her father and brother-in-law. She would have enjoyed the sense of satisfaction she got from looking down on the shops and the people and the tall Roman columns on the Via Augustan. But today, she barely glanced at the scene.

She reached the grove of tamarisks, lush with foliage, and pushed far back into them, seeking her safest refuge in their densest growth. Once there, she flopped to the ground exhausted. Her breath came and went in short, pain-racked bursts. Her heart pounded fast, loud, causing her to tremble. She hugged herself in an effort to slow her runaway heart and soothe the painful breathing. She lay back full length on the ground and wiped at her eyes with a bruised hand. One eye felt puffy. She knew it would swell shut, just like it had the last time Coniah had beaten her.

Why did she stay with him? Why did she put up with such abuse? Was this all she could ever expect from life? Was no man to ever really love her, or be gentle with her, or care for her? The questions went through her mind as they had a thousand other times. And as they had a thousand other times, they remained unanswered.

But the next question which came to mind had an immediate answer. Why had she married Coniah in the first place? The answer was one she knew by heart. It was one which made her feel helpless and hopeless. Her marriage to Coniah had been arranged, as had her other four marriages. It was the custom. Coniah had paid her father the most handsome of all the dowries. It was even more handsome than that of her first marriage when she was a virgin.

"It's a good business arrangement," her father had said. "It fulfills the ancient Samaritan custom. More than that, it solves the very large question of 'How do we eat?' "

She understood. Her father was so poor he earned barely enough to feed and shelter himself and her mother, Yasmin. Many slaves lived better than they did. When she had returned to his house upon the death of her fourth husband, her father's situation became desperate. He quickly searched for yet another husband for this ill-fated daughter.

He found Coniah, a muleteer with a heavy money pouch and a yen to marry. He negotiated the handsome dowry. But in the process, her father failed to mention that misfortune had trailed this daughter, the second of two female children, since her birth; and that she had been married to four other men. Not long after the marriage ceremony, Coniah learned of the previous marriages, realized he'd paid a dowry much too high, and flew into a rage.

"You never told me she'd been married before," Coniah shouted at her father. "She's three times a widow and once abandoned. You've cheated me, you son of a jackal!"

Hassad pleaded to a misunderstanding and fled to the safety of the Tetrarch's olive groves. By the time he returned, Coniah had turned on Mara as a more satisfying target for his anger. After that, he beat her often. She feared and despised him; thought often of running away from him. But always, she was stopped by the greater fear of not knowing where she could go, or who would take care of her, or how she would survive.

She sat up, realizing again she had nowhere to turn. She had few friends, none of whom could really help her. Nor did she have relatives who would help. Aside from her parents and sister, there was only one cousin still alive. She was considerably older. Her name was Nehushta. She lived in Sychar. And Sychar was more than a day's journey to the east from Sebaste. She had not seen Nehushta for many years. Even though she remembered her as a kind person, it would be silly to expect help from someone she barely knew.

The old, familiar questions repeated themselves in her mind. How could she get away from Coniah? Where could she go? Who would take care of her? She hugged her knees to her chest and rocked back and forth, considering her future.

Her mother might want to help. But her father would not allow it. She doubted that going again to Timna and Tabeal would bring her any comfort. They had their own lives to live. They'd made that plain when she had gone to them some time earlier.

"You know we cannot help you," her brother-in-law, Tabeal, complained. "We have to get along with your father."

"Our father would not help you even if he was not poor, and not afraid of Coniah," Timna reminded her. "He hates it that we are daughters. You know that."

Mara nodded. "How could I forget it? Our very names remind me. At least you were given a name with a decent meaning."

Timna objected. "You think a name meaning 'restraint' is decent?"

"It's better than mine! Mara! 'Bitter.' " She spat out the name and its meaning. Like everything else about her life, she disliked her name. "'Bitter'! My name makes me feel like what it means! Toward our father. Toward everything."

Tabeal laughed. "How do you think your father feels? Why do you think he gave you that name? He put your mother away from himself because she gave him no sons. He felt disgraced that he had no sons." He laughed again, sneering. "Besides, Mara, your name suits you. Nothing but bitter misfortune has ever followed you."

"Tabeal!"

"Mara is bad luck," he insisted, ignoring his wife's objection. "Every man who ever married her had bitter misfortune."

The truth of his words was hard.

"I want none of your misfortune." He motioned for her to leave. "Bad luck hangs about you like a shroud, Mara. Begone!"

She could not argue with him. Even if he had been wrong, she could not have argued with him. But he was not wrong. A deep and hurtful sadness came over her. Bad luck did cling to her. She'd never understood why. She understood only the pain of it and the awful weight of rejection that it brought.

Just remembering the rejection was a burden. She laid back down in her hiding place thinking about her burden, and about Tabeal and Timna, about her relationship with her parents, and about all the misfortune which had pursued each of her previous marriages.

She was, indeed, misfortune's target. As much, and as often, as she had prayed to the great One God, nothing had changed that fact. Her prayers had gone unanswered. She was misfortune's target. Her life with her husbands showed how true that was.

Peresh, a musician, her first husband, had abandoned her. Her second husband, Harsha, a worker in ivory, died of a fever. Her third husband, Gaal, was a soldier conscripted by the Romans and was killed in a fight. Jered, a goatherder, was her fourth husband. He had died from injuries sustained in a fall.

Three times a widow and once abandoned, and she had yet to see her twenty-fourth winter. In her widowhood, she did not even have the solace of having borne a child. People jeered, laughed, ridiculed her barrenness. And now she was married to Coniah. More misfortune, and more unanswered prayers. For her, it seemed to be just as she had heard it read from the sacred scroll, "The Lord God said, Woman, I will greatly multiply thy sorrow — and thy husband shall rule over thee."

She hid her face in her hands and wept in desolation. Why did everything seem to go against her? Why was it always her fault when things went wrong? Why had no one ever really loved her? Why had she been unable to really care for someone else? What was it like to love someone? Would the feeling ever be hers?

There must be someone to turn to. Somewhere. There must be someone who could help her. Sometime. But who? And where? And when?

Like the question about why she stayed with Coniah, these questions, too, seemed to have no answers. Street sounds drifted up from the Via Augustan, distracting her. She lifted her face from her hands, wiped at her eyes and looked about. The puffy eye was now swollen shut, but with her good eye she could see the wind teasing the tamarisks with restless frustration.

The wind brought the street sounds up to her more clearly. They were the sounds of a caravan moving along the Via Augustan. It was a common enough sound in a city like Sebaste. By Roman standards, Sebaste was an important city, boasting a temple, a mausoleum, a hippodrome, a theatre, and a palace. Its population was a rich mix of Babylonians, Greeks, Arabs, Idumeans,

Moabites, Romans, and Samaritans like herself. Caravans, large and small, came and went at all hours. Why should the sounds of this particular caravan stir so strangely in her mind?

Then she remembered. Earlier, she had heard a legionnaire haggling with Coniah over what he would charge to take a herd of pack mules to the Roman garrison in Caesarea-by-the-Sea.

Was Coniah with the caravan now moving on the street below? Had he given up the search for her? Had she been in hiding longer than she realized? She glanced at the sky. The sun was almost to its western edge. Great shadows were lengthening all around her. She got up, walked to the edge of the precipice and scanned the crowded scene below.

Most of the caravan already had passed through the city gate and was tracking northwestward on the road to Caesarea-by-the-Sea. Near the rear of the procession, she could pick out the pack mules and Coniah. Even at this distance, her fear of him recaptured her. She trembled. One day Coniah would kill her. She knew it in her bones. Unless, of course, she killed him first. He was brutish and cruel. It was now clearly dangerous for her to live with him any longer.

She wished him dead. He deserved to die. She began to wonder if she could kill him, and how she might go about it. It would not be with force. She could never overpower him. She wondered if she could poison him, and almost as quickly, rejected that idea, too. She had no money to buy poison.

How could she protect herself from him? On her own, she had no legal rights to claim for protection.

Only men could claim such rights. It was the custom. It was the law. She also realized once again that there was no one in all of the city of Sebaste to help her. She was alone with her problem. She would have to find her own solution. She was certain of only one thing: Never again would she allow Coniah to touch her.

But how could she stop him? How could she get away from him? And even if she could, where could she go?

The last of the pack mules passed through the city's western gate. As it closed behind them, she realized Coniah could not beat her now. Until he returned to Sebaste, she need have no fear of him. In relief, she sighed. Her trembling stopped, and she began to think more clearly about what she should do.

The first thing to be done, she told herself, was to get down from this place. Precarious as the trail was in daylight, darkness would make it doubly so. She stepped back from the precipice and cautiously retraced her steps through the rocky overgrowth. By the time she arrived again amid the squalid houses of her neighbors, full darkness was upon the city. Only the sputtering amber glow of the neighbors' cookfires disrupted it.

Inside Coniah's house, the darkness deepened to unrelenting blackness. The cookfire had long since grown cold. She stopped just inside the doorway, trying to remember where she'd put the small tallow oil lamp, and letting her one good eye adjust itself to the dark.

She stood there in the blackness and the silence realizing that it was the first time she had never been afraid in this house. Coniah was gone. And he would be gone for at least two days, the length of the journey to Caesarea with a herd of pack mules.

She began to count on her fingers. "Two days' journey to get to Caesarea-by-the-Sea. Two days' journey to come back, plus however many days he will stay in that city." She hesitated, but only for a moment, as the thought of Coniah's stinginess came to her. "He will only stay three days. After that, he would have to pay his host."

She ran the numbers across her fingers again. Two. Two. And three. Seven days. Coniah could be away for as many as seven days. That was plenty of time to decide about her own future. On the other hand, Coniah was so unpredictable that he might return much sooner. An odd sensation of warning went through her. She must not tarry over her decision. She must decide soon. She felt it in her bones.

As her one good eye finally adjusted itself to the blackness in the house, she could make out the dim forms of the table and bench, and beyond, the flat stack of sleeping mats. Opposite was a small chest containing a scanty supply of foodstuffs: cheeses, bread, some olives in a pottery crock. A goatskin filled with water rested on top of the chest.

"Everything belongs to Coniah," she said out loud. "Nothing here is mine. Nothing. I have nothing. I am nothing. And no one cares."

It was then she remembered the shawl and the beaded doll. She did have something that belonged to her after all. How could she have forgotten these treasures? She had hidden them behind the loose bricks near the doorway when she'd first come to Coniah's house. But she still treasured them.

How could she have forgotten them, even for a moment? Her mother had made the doll for her. It was her only childhood toy and remained a cherished sign of the only family affection she'd ever really known. The shawl, on the other hand, had been a gift from Cousin Nehushta when she moved from Sebaste to Sychar many years before.

Cousin Nehushta!

Maybe Cousin Nehushta in Sychar would help her after all.

Her thoughts suddenly connected with the old questions in her mind. Maybe Cousin Nehushta would give her safe refuge in Sychar. Maybe this was the solution to the problems that plagued her.

Excited at this new thought, she knelt down, groped for the loosened bricks, and pulled her family treasures from their hiding place. The doll was wrapped inside the shawl. She had placed it there herself. Now it seemed symbolic somehow, as if a part of her child-hood innocence was still protected from the awful reality of life.

In Cousin Nehushta she could find a friend. In Sychar she could find safety. She began to tremble in anticipation and unwrapped the shawl until her fingers touched the doll. Even in the darkness, she knew its every detail. It was small, tattered, unbeautiful, but treasured for the value of a past kindness. Now, she regarded it with even more value. Now, she felt it was an omen for her future.

In a spasm of hope, she wept tears of relief and pressed the shawl and the doll close to her bosom as if cradling a precious new life.

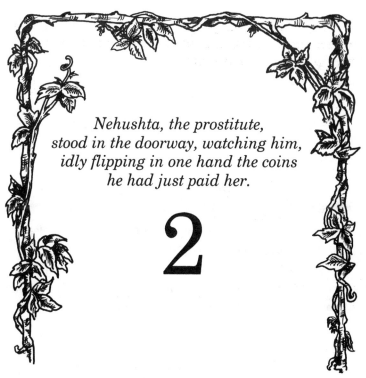

*Nehushta, the prostitute,
stood in the doorway, watching him,
idly flipping in one hand the coins
he had just paid her.*

2

THE VILLAGE OF SYCHAR was known for three things—its location, a well, and a town official named Benoni-bar-Micah.

In truth, the location and the well were far better known than was Benoni. Even he admitted that. It could scarcely be otherwise, since it was Sychar's location and the nearby well which had caused him to be sent here from his beloved island of Delos. But he'd never liked it. Still didn't after three years. And he especially didn't like it on this day, and at this particular moment.

He hesitated outside the doorway of the house of Nehushta, the prostitute, and glanced back.

She stood in the doorway, watching him, idly flipping in one hand the coins he had just paid to her.

Anger rose inside him. Each time he went to her, it cost him more—and the satisfaction he felt grew less. "You are well-named, Nehushta. A piece of brass!" he called out to her. "You are like that. Like your name. A piece of brass!"

She straightened.

A man passing by overheard, laughed and made an ugly gesture to Nehushta.

"You are hard and cold," Benoni added. "You give no more than a piece of brass could give."

Her face darkened. She stepped aside and slammed the door shut. Its wooden panels shuddered. Dust rose from the threshold in a shower of agitation.

He turned away, cursing, pulled a money pouch from the leather girdle at his waist, and emptied it into the palm of his hand. There was barely enough left to buy bread and cheese, let alone a flagon of balsam rum. He cursed again, replaced the coins, stuffed the pouch into his tunic and walked on down the ugly, dusty street.

He needed a woman of his own; a woman like Lioda who had lived with him on Delos. She had kept his house, washed his clothes, done his cooking, and given herself to him whenever he asked. He hadn't loved her, but he missed her. She was warm and soft and giving.

During his time in Sychar, he had not found anyone quite like her. Not even his position as a scribe in the employ of the Tetrarch Herod Antipas had helped him attract such a woman. Occasionally he hired local girls to keep his house. But to satisfy his need for a woman's company, he visited Nehushta. "That piece of brass!" he muttered, hating the fate that had caused him to be sent to this alien place.

Sychar was the administrative center for Herod Antipas's toparchy of eastern Samarian and western Perean settlements with populations of 15,000 or less. Even though Samaria and Perea, like Judea, were under the jurisdiction of Rome, the toparchies and other political structures set up by Antipas's father, Herod the Great, had been left intact. It was a political gesture from Rome's Emperor Tiberius Caesar to Herod Antipas. It symbolized Antipas's importance to Rome.

Sychar was a natural choice as an administrative center since it was located at the crossing point of two important roadways through Samaria's rugged hill country. The north-south road connected Galilee and other northern provinces with Jerusalem. The east-west road wound through the narrow valley separating the holy mountains of Ebal and Gerizim, giving travelers access westward to Samaria's capital city of Sebaste, and to the Great Sea beyond. Eastward, the road led to the River Jordan and across it to the territory of Perea where another important north-south road connected Galilee and the other northern provinces to Jerusalem.

The Perean road was a longer and rougher trail. But it was the most popular north-south route for Jews since it did not go through Samaria. Jews and Samaritans had hated one another since the ancient days when certain Israelites intermarried with the conquering Assyrian invaders. When the Jews returned from their exile in Babylon and began to rebuild the ruined Temple of Solomon in Jerusalem, the

Samaritans offered to help. Their help was contemptuously refused on the grounds that Samaritans were crossbred, and therefore, Levitically unclean.

The insult was never forgotten, nor forgiven. A rival temple was built on Mount Gerizim. And Jews traveled through Samaria at risk of being waylaid and maltreated.

Benoni found the whole idea of feuding over something as nebulous as religion a waste of time. For him, the pantheon of Roman gods was a far more practical sort of belief. Roman gods required no pilgrimages. Nor did they demand rituals of washing hands and feet, separating eating utensils for meat dishes and milk dishes or demand special favor of a person. Roman gods expected a man to do his work and live his life. They were practical gods. A man could call on whichever one he needed at any given moment. Yes, Benoni had long since decided that feuding over religion was foolish.

On the other hand, he sorely resented the fact that the effects of the religious feud were still being felt in his own time, and in his own job. No road tax was being collected on the Perean road. Removal of the tax had been ordered by Herod Antipas some years before in order to encourage Jews to make more pilgrimages to Jerusalem without having to travel through Samaritan territory.

In Benoni's opinion it was an impractical order. And it cut into his own purse, since toparchy scribes earned a percentage of the total tax collected within their districts. He had already decided to try to get the tax reinstated. Within the next two or three days, he planned to travel to Tiberias and talk with the Roman commander there. The commander owed him a favor.

In the meantime, he diligently collected taxes on the roads located near Sychar and its famous Well of Jacob. The ancient well made the whole area important to travelers, particularly to military convoys and commercial caravans. The life-giving waters sustained both man and his animals. Cool and pure, the waters had existed as long as the holy mountains of Ebal and Gerizim, and sprang from some cavernous source deep within the earth. All who drank of them considered the well to be a vital gift of God.

So far as Benoni-bar-Micah was concerned, however, he could think of no one who considered him a gift from God, vital or otherwise. As Herod Antipas's official in this place, he was the least popular of all men. Of that, he was certain. His duties not only included collection of taxes, but also the posting of official notices in public places, preparation of trade and travel documents, and the reading and writing of letters for all citizens. This latter duty was supposed to be done without charge.

But if the customer was not a citizen of Sychar, Benoni did charge for this service. It was his own decision. He felt entitled to the extra money. So far, no one had complained. No one questioned his right to do it, apparently considering it a natural act for a self-important little man.

Natural act or not, he kept the extra money and ignored those who thought of him as a self-important little man. What he could not ignore, however, was the fact that he was barely tall enough to see over the back of a mule when standing beside it, and that his weight considerably exceeded the limits of his small frame. In spite of this, he thought of himself as physically tough, and he still moved with the characteristic haste of his younger days.

Considering his occupations, this was fortunate. In addition to his official duties, Benoni conducted a side-line business of forgery. He was skillful at it, but then forgery was a long-familiar activity for him. He had learned it from his father, Micah, who had been an overseer of warehouses for Herod Antipas on Delos. When Micah died, Benoni had been appointed his successor.

It seemed only appropriate to continue the practice of forgery as well. It put more money in his purse than did the wage he earned from Herod Antipas. When he was ordered to move to Sychar, it was easy to take the skill with him. His most recent forgery was for a Roman officer who had not liked his newest assignment and had come to him for a set of different orders. He had obliged for a nice price, and there was yet a future profit to be made from it. If all things were right, and the gods were with him, his most recent forgery might well turn out to be his most profitable. Bringing the skill of forgery with him was a smart thing as well as an easy thing to do.

Other aspects of the move had not been as easy. Like having to leave Lioda behind on Delos. He turned into the street where the cheesemaker lived, telling himself again that he really did need to find a woman of his own. For another thing, he needed to find a different house. The one he had was cramped and small, jammed close between three others. There was no view. No view at all. On Delos, he had lived in a house with a view of the sea. He missed having a view. He missed the sea.

He closed his eyes for a moment, remembering the taste of its salt in the air and the feel of its dampness in the mists of morning. He still longed for it, especially when the khamsin, the east winds from the deserts of Arabia, cast a shroud of sand over the land and all that moved on it. He opened his eyes and cast a look skyward, knowing that khamsin soon would come, and hating it.

Samaria was a harsh land with only two seasons, winter and summer. The winters were wet and cold and the summers hot and dry. They were separated only by strange transitional periods when the khamsin, the east winds, devastated the landscape and all its inhabitants. Samaria's people were harsh, too. Harsh, and with few exceptions, unyielding; cold and hard. Pieces of brass, like Nehushta. He spat into the dusty street, trying to rid himself of the bitter taste of the place and her people.

He turned into the last alleyway before the cheese-maker's house. Even as he did so, the reek of curdled milk assailed him. He held his nose and went inside. The cheesemaker stood in the center of the room at a small table, wrapping several cheeses in thin cloth. Glancing up, he barely nodded, and went on with his work.

"You have a cheese to sell?"

The man gestured to the cheeses already wrapped.

"How much for this one?"

"Five leptons."

"For this small cheese?" Benoni objected, releasing his nose for a moment.

"Five leptons."

He wondered why he liked cheese to eat when the place where it was made always smelled so bad. "I'll give you two leptons."

"I have a wife and many children," the cheesemaker complained. "The cheese is worth five leptons."

"Two is all I can pay," Benoni insisted. "And I am in a hurry."

The cheesemaker shrugged and turned away.

Benoni moved closer to the table and fingered a cheese larger than the one he originally had indicated. "And I am Herod's scribe," he added, staring straight at the cheesemaker's back.

When the man glanced around in surprise, Benoni met the glance with an unwavering stare, and pointed to the royal signet of his office that hung pendant-like at his neck on a thin leather cord.

The cheesemaker returned to the table and peered nearsightedly at the royal signet.

Benoni waited for him to understand its importance.

"The cheese is worth five leptons," the man said in a slow, calculating tone.

Still, Benoni waited.

The cheesemaker cocked his head to one side. "Herod's scribe?"

Benoni nodded, still staring at him.

For a moment's more hesitation, the cheesemaker seemed to consider the situation; then yielded. "Give me three leptons, and I will sell the cheese for that pittance."

Benoni already had the money pouch in his hand and was counting out the three bronze Greek coins. He gave them to the man, and grinned at the thought that his position with Herod did carry importance in small things.

His next stop was at the house of the widow Hodesh to buy bread. The widow was absent, a fact he considered fortunate, not wanting to listen to her gossip. Instead, her daughter sold him one of the brown, round loaves in silence.

He quickly went on to the house of his friend, Matri, the town elder. Matri also sold the balsam rum brought up from Jericho.. He discovered that the wooden gate to Matri's house was closed and tightly latched. Wondering why, he juggled the bread and cheese into the crook of one arm and loudly rapped at the gate with his free hand. He could hear no sound of movement on the other side of the gate; but he waited, aware that Matri moved slowly. So did his wife, Shua. In all likelihood, Shua was at the well drawing water for the night.

While he waited he glanced skyward, seeking the telltale yellow that preceded the arrival of the khamsin. But there was none yet. The late afternoon was blue and clear with not even one wandering cloud in sight. Growing impatient, he rapped again at the gate – this time more demandingly. At last he heard the old man's shuffling footsteps and the sound of the latch being unbolted.

"Enter, Benoni. Enter, my friend."

Benoni stepped into the small, neat courtyard, and salaamed. A single hibiscus bush bloomed red and lush in one corner. A small cook-oven, made of the usual mud-bricks, was nearby. Beyond was a trough for water and hay for Matri's donkey. The droppings from the donkey had been swept into a neat pile to dry before being used as fuel for the cooking fire. The donkey was absent, a fact which further convinced Benoni that Shua had, indeed, gone to the well. In recent months she had taken the donkey with her more and more often to carry the heavy waterskins back to the village.

"Welcome to my home, my friend." Matri pointed to the bread and cheese. "From the look of it, you're in need of a flagon of balsam rum."

"You have a supply to sell to me?"

"I do," Matri said, turning back toward the house. "Our friend, Rakem, returned from Jericho only a short time ago with a new supply. He is still here, helping me store the casks in a place where the Romans won't think to look."

"That is good," Benoni said, understanding now why the gate had been closed and latched. "That is very good, in fact. If the Romans can't find the rum, I won't have to collect an extra tax on it, will I? The price I pay you for it will be less, and your profit will be more. Let the Romans take the loss, eh?"

"That would be my thought and my hope," the old man chuckled, leading the way into the house.

Benoni followed. Rakem, Matri and Shua were the only real friends he had been able to make since coming to Sychar. They were different from the other people in the village. He didn't know exactly why they were different. He'd wondered about it a lot. Sometimes he thought it was because of their religious beliefs. They prayed a lot. They talked a lot about God. And once when the Passover time came, they had invited him to go with them to the altar on the top of Mount Gerizim for the ceremony. He went but understood nothing about it, and wished he had saved himself the walk and the climb. Afterward, though, he kept remembering the looks of radiance he'd seen on their faces as they worshipped and prayed that day. He wondered about that, too; tried often to imagine what kind of feelings could be experienced that would cause such looks of radiance, such looks of joy and satisfaction. Maybe one day he would talk about it with Matri.

"Look who has come to sample the rum, Rakem," Matri called out when they entered the hidden storeroom.

The young man stacking the last of several casks turned and grinned at Benoni. His eyes were a piercing light blue in color and contrasted oddly with the darkness of his skin. "Have you come to drink with us? Or buy from us? Or have you come to make your tax books look fatter?"

"That depends on how much news you have brought back from Jericho."

"Some of the news I bring may affect you, my friend."

Matri intervened, motioning to two reed-thatched stools. Benoni moved one for the old man to sit on and took the other for himself.

Rakem sat down on one of the casks. "Herod Antipas is leaving his winter palace at Jericho . . . "

"There's no news in that, Rakem," Benoni interrupted. "It is the season for him to move into the palace at either Sebaste or at Sepphoris."

Rakem's piercing blue eyes darkened a bit. "Not this time. He's moving his royal entourage to the fortress Machaerus across the Jordan."

"Machaerus?"

"Machaerus?" Matri echoed. "But that's halfway down the distance of the Dead Sea. It is even warmer there than in Jericho at this time of the year. Why Machaerus?"

"And why should such a move affect me?" Benoni asked with a laugh. "Machaerus is on the southern boundary of Perea."

"So it is. But my friends in Jericho tell me that's where Herod is going, and that he will call together all the scribes from his toparchies in Perea, in Galilee, and in Samaria. It will affect you, my friend."

The sincerity with which Rakem said this sent a curious sensation of wariness through Benoni. He disliked change. Especially change affecting his job. And especially when the news of it came from an unofficial source, even Rakem. "Why should Herod call all his scribes together in Machaerus?"

"For an accounting of some kind."

Benoni tensed.

Matri turned, questioning him with a concerned look. "An accounting?"

"My Jericho friends tell me there is even more to it than that," Rakem went on. "They tell me the real reason Herod is leaving Jericho is to get himself and his new wife, Herodias, away from the man called John the Baptizer. And away from all the public outrage that the Baptizer's preaching is bringing down on him.

Benoni relaxed. The name meant nothing to him.

But Matri straightened abruptly. "And what of the Nazarene? Is Herod frightened of him, too?"

Curious as he was at Matri's reaction, this name meant nothing to Benoni, either.

"It is just as you predicted," Rakem said. "Herod's divorce from the Nabatean woman, and his marriage to the wife of his half-brother, is causing public strife all over the land. The Nazarene is speaking out against the divorce and marriage, too. His words are different. But his meaning is the same."

Both men lapsed into a thoughtful silence.

For only the second time since he'd become friends with these two men, Benoni felt alone in their presence. He'd had a similar feeling when he was with them at the Passover ceremony atop Mount Gerizim the year before. It was as if they both knew all about some important subject that he knew nothing about. He didn't like the feeling. It was uncomfortable. He felt like an intruder. He started to get up off the reed stool, but Matri's next words made him hesitate.

"If John is baptizing near Jericho again, he must be near the place where he baptized the Nazarene."

Rakem nodded. "And he is drawing larger crowds than when we were there. He is preaching about the sin of divorce and the sin of lust. He is reminding everyone of the great commandments which Moses brought down to Sinai. And he is preaching about these things less than two miles from the gate of Herod's palace in Jericho. Think of the courage John must have!"

Matri turned to Benoni. "It may seem strange to you, my friend, that we Samaritans are so interested in a Jew who lives in the wilderness and preaches repentance."

"And that's what this man named John does?" Benoni asked. "But where does he come from? Who is he?"

"He comes from the desert, so far as anyone can know."

"He wears a camel-hair cloak with a waist belt of leather. He is bearded, and wild-looking."

"It is said he lives on locusts and wild honey," Rakem said. "But he may well be the herald that is to come before our Messiah."

Benoni guessed that his face must have shown the surprise he felt, for Matri hurried on with a further explanation.

"In spite of all the hatred and the mistrust between us and the Jews, both Samaritans and Jews believe deeply in the great sacred scroll. Jews call it the Torah. We share a common belief in the One True God. We share a common belief that a messiah, a savior, is destined to come and free us.

"And you think this John the Baptizer is your messiah?"

"Some people do," Rakem said. "Both Jews and Samaritans."

"What do you think?"

"I think as Matri does that John the Baptizer is the herald who has come to prepare the way for the Messiah."

Benoni was fascinated that these two men, men he'd grown to like and trust and thought he'd learned to know, were so wrapped up in the belief of One True God and One True Messiah. Their sincerity was obvious. And yet, he knew that the entire world outside of the village of Sychar believed no such thing. There were hundreds of gods. A man could pick and choose. It surprised him that Matri and Rakem didn't know this. And as for some man coming along to free them, how could they, as intelligent men, believe such a thing? It had to be a myth. What man could save the world? Especially that part of the world owned by the Romans?

"How do you know that this John the Baptizer is not your messiah?" he hesitantly asked.

"Because he tells us so."

"And that is your proof?"

"No proof is needed, if a man's word is good," Matri said quietly. "We believe John the Baptizer is a prophet. He preaches that he only baptizes with water, but that one greater than he is to come who will baptize with the Spirit."

Benoni glanced from one to the other of his friends, wondering at their innocence, questioning their gullibility, trying to make sense of it all, and finally deciding that something political was involved in all this talk. But what kind of politics? Perplexed, he shook his head.

Of far greater importance to him, and of much more immediate concern, was the news Rakem had brought about Herod Antipas ordering his scribes to come together at the fortress Machaerus. Whether or not it was a ploy to hide the Tetrarch's escape from the preachings of a wild man, the meeting was potentially dangerous for any scribe whose records and tax scrolls were not complete and accurate. In his own case, additional danger might be lurking in the fact that he was so accomplished at forgery as well.

He stood up, and pulled his money pouch from his tunic. "How much of the rum can I buy from you, my friends?"

"Will two flagons be all right?" Matri asked, getting to his feet.

Benoni nodded and handed the old man the usual number of coins. He returned the money pouch to his tunic and picked up the bread and cheese.

Rakem turned toward the casks, opened one and poured an amount equal to two flagons into a new wineskin.

"Did your Jericho friends tell you when Herod will call together all the scribes?" Benoni took the wineskin from Rakem.

"Within a very few days, apparently."

Benoni thanked him, made the customary salaam to Matri, and left his friends. There was much to do to prepare for such a journey as described by Rakem. And the first thing to do was to make certain his records and tax scrolls were accurate to the last lepton.

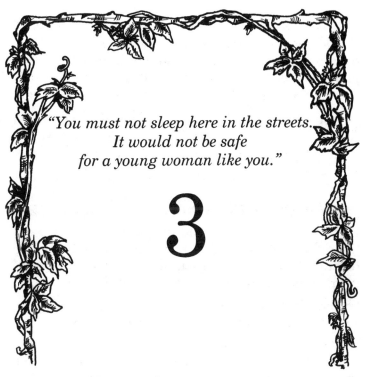

"You must not sleep here in the streets.
It would not be safe
for a young woman like you."

3

FROM THE MOMENT of her decision to leave Samaria, Mara had felt like a different woman. She was trembling with anticipation, and a little frightened at the prospect of going out into the world all alone. But, she reminded herself, she was alone in Sebaste, even if her family was still there. She was also in danger in Sebaste. Or would be when Coniah returned.

At least now she was on her way to a new life. There might be other dangers that she'd never thought of. Whatever they might be, she could not imagine how they could be worse than the life she was leaving.

She had rewrapped the doll in the shawl, gathered a cheese, a loaf of bread and a small skin of water, put on the only cloak she possessed, and left the house of Coniah forever. She found a small, sheltered niche near Sebaste's eastern gate. There she slept until the earliest pre-dawn light began to show itself, and the gatekeeper was roused by an incoming caravan to open the portal.

As the caravan came into Sebaste, she slipped unseen out and away from the city. To the east she would come to Sychar and find her cousin Nehushta.

The countryside lay cloaked in the uncertainty of earliest daylight. The air was cold, frosty. Even with her own cloak pulled close around her, its chill touched her, made her shiver. She found the roadway rough. Sand filtered into her sandals. Unobserved stones caused her to stumble. Her belongings, meager as they were, quickly grew heavy, and she began to doubt the wisdom of her journey.

Yet she would not turn back. She could not. To retrace her steps would be the sheerest of folly and against whatever good reason she could muster. By the time the sun rose high enough to remove the shadowy cloak of dawn, Sebaste lay out of sight behind her, its walls hidden by the intervening hills.

On the road in front of her, a small caravan approached, heading for Sebaste. A man on horseback came first. He was followed by four men on foot carrying a small litter. Another man on horseback, two pack animals and their drovers brought up the rear of the procession.

Mara stepped off the roadway and waited for them to pass. As they did, she saw that a woman rode in the litter. She was dressed in a beautiful woolen cloak. The shawl placed about her head was ornate with embroidery, and her face was veiled in the custom for all women of wealth and importance.

A pang of admiration mixed with jealousy went through Mara. She wondered what it might be like to have wealth, to be important. For one thing, her father would have to respect her. Tabeal and Timna would have to pay homage to her. And as for Coniah — with wealth or importance, she could certainly deal with him. She could afford to hire someone to beat him, or poison him, or kill him. The mere thought of it brought her pleasure.

The small caravan faded into the distance toward Sebaste. She shifted the burden of her belongings from one arm to the other and moved eastward once more. The power of wealth would never be hers. She knew that. "I am nothing," she whispered to herself. "And it will always be so. I know it in my bones."

She glanced skyward in a gesture of submission. It was a characteristic motion. She did it without thinking. Her entire life had been an act of submission and misfortune. As a child, she had submitted to her mother's wish that she help nurse Timna through a sickness. She caught the disease herself and was left with the unattractive pock-marks on her face. Timna had none. When her father had insisted that she marry her first husband, Peresh, she had not resisted, though she knew that he didn't love or want her and that he probably would abandon her. When he did, she was blamed for it, accused of chasing him away. With the deaths of her second, third and fourth husbands, she had submitted to her father's anger and accepted his opinion that she'd somehow been responsible for their deaths. She began to believe it. In her heart she harbored the certainty that there was something about her which caused misfortune, even death, to manifest itself in her life. It was as if some spirit always huddled near her, waiting for the moment of uncertainty or danger to release misfortune on her, or on those who were close to her. Tabeal had been right. She did wear misfortune like a shroud.

How could she be otherwise than submissive, she asked herself, tossing another glance of supplication skyward. A yellowish cast had appeared in the southeast and was filtering over the clear colors of morning, dulling them. Khamsin. Soon, a pall of yellow would close out the world around her. All of it. Even the warmth of the sun would be affected. Bitter dust would take command of the roadway, meld it into the surrounding landscape, and cause travelers to lose their way. Khamsin. Any creature caught out in the open, without shelter, would become a victim of the scouring sand; be left with skin flayed and pitted and with air too heavy with grit for breathing. Grit everywhere. In eyes, mouth, nose. Khamsin.

A panicky feeling went through her. She must find shelter, and quickly. Ahead of her, and off to the right of the roadway, she saw a small group of trees. Behind them, the land inclined upward for a short distance, creating a shield against the coming winds. She hurried in that direction.

At the base of the incline of land were a number of large rocks thrown there randomly by the great unseen hand of nature. But at one place, the rocks were positioned in such a way as to form a shallow cave. It was all the protection she would need, provided some other creature had not already claimed the spot.

She searched about for a short stick, found one, and poked it into the opening in a sweeping motion. No creature came scurrying out. The shelter was hers to occupy. She got down on her hands and knees, pushed her small bundle of belongings into the space, and crawled in after it.

Now, khamsin could vent its fury. She was protected. A sense of well-being began to settle over her and the chill from the morning air left her. She snuggled against the treasured shawl, careful not to injure the doll so lovingly wrapped inside, and soon fell asleep.

Sometime later she awakened, unsure of what had disturbed her, unsure of where she was, but alert and sensing danger. Then she remembered, leaned up onto one elbow and looked outside her shelter. She saw nothing other than blowing sand. She heard no sound save the screech of the khamsin.

Had she been dreaming? she asked herself. Had fear awakened her because of a dream? Or was the sense of danger real and from a source other than Coniah? She waited – listening, looking. Nothing alien moved. Satisfied that no creature stirred close to her shelter, she laid back, resettled herself next to her bundle and once more fell asleep.

When next she awoke, khamsin had blown itself out. The yowling screech of the wind had stopped. She sat up and looked out. A new day revealed a landscape altered by drifts and dunes. The trees just in front of her shelter were adorned with great skirts of sand piled up where the trees themselves had blocked khamsin's onslaught.

She rubbed at her eyes. The puffiness in the one eye had lessened enough for her to see out of it again. But her throat was dry, her lips parched with grit. And hunger growled in her belly. She reached for the waterskin, pulled its stopper and sipped a small amount, then cupped one hand and poured another small amount to splash over her face.

It felt good. She rubbed her face and the back of her neck with her wet hand. It was refreshing and comforting all at the same time.

For a moment, she wondered why water had such a reviving effect. There was nothing else quite like it. No wonder the priests always read so much from the sacred scroll about water, she thought. It was surely the one thing life must have.

She put the stopper back onto the waterskin, unwrapped the bread and cheese, and ate. Hunger satisfied, she rewrapped the bread and cheese and packed them and the waterskin into one bundle with her doll and shawl. Then, pushing the bundle in front of her, she crawled out of the sheltered place.

She stood and stretched, easing muscles that had been cramped for too long, and more carefully scanned the altered landscape. The roadway had disappeared beneath a ridged length of sand. No creature, animal or human, was in sight. A thin yellow haze clung to the dome of sky, an after-threat of khamsin which allowed only the merest penetration of sunlight.

Uncertainty gripped her. In which direction should she travel? She shielded her eyes with her hand and peered into the distance. Gradually, she made out the shape of two far-away prominences. Their shapes were different from all other surrounding hills. They had to be Mount Ebal and Mount Gerizim, she decided. Her feeling of uncertainty lifted. She had heard them described and talked about since her childhood. She knew people in Sebaste who had made pilgrimages to them. Her family never had, of course.

"Too poor," her father had always whined.

Too poor, indeed. She was too poor to make the trip also. But necessity pushed her to seek sanctuary near the holy mountains. Sychar, a place of safety. Cousin Nehushta, a friend. She shifted her bundle and set out, using the tops of the holy mountains as her guide.

By the time afternoon waned toward nightfall, Mara was more than halfway through the narrow valley intervening between the holy mountains. On both sides of the road were fields of corn. In the cup-shaped valley before her, she saw a crossroads where a throng of people and animals had converged, as if at a watering place. A few trees clustered near the spot. Just beyond, on the eastern slope of Mount Gerizim, clustered the buildings of Sychar.

She hurried forward to fill her almost-empty waterskin before going on to the village. A babble of voices came to her, confusing her ears with languages she didn't know. There were others, however, that she did recognize—the flat, rough dialect of Galilee, the rhythmic cadence of Aramaic, and the harsh, blunt Greek used by the Romans.

The crowd was large. She had to wait her turn to fill her waterskin. Men had first chance for themselves, second chance for their thirsty animals. Then the women crowded forward. Mara hung back, for she now could see that the well was deep and she had nothing to draw water with.

"Misfortune again," she muttered. "Always misfortune. Why me?"

Two women carrying freshly filled waterpots on their shoulders edged their way back from the well, struggling against those who surged forward to take their places. As they passed by Mara, one of them tripped over the long cord tied to the handle of her waterpot and stumbled. Her waterpot tipped, fell from her shoulder and crashed to the ground, breaking into several pieces. As the water raced from the pot to freedom on the thirsty ground, Mara scrambled forward. She grabbed the pot's broken handle with its cord attached and scurried away with it.

Behind a small bush at the far edge of the crowd, she untied the cord from the piece of broken pot and attached it to her own waterskin. Now she had something to draw water with. This time fortune was on her side.

Her confidence rising, she made sure the woman whose cord she'd stolen had left, then went back to the well. Carefully she laid aside her bundle, took the stopper from the waterskin and, holding tightly to the stolen cord, lowered the container into the well.

There was only the shortest length of cord left in her now-trembling hands when she heard the waterskin plop into the water deep below. It quickly grew heavy as it filled. She clutched more tightly to the cord and began to pull it up out of the well. She put the stopper back in, picked up her burden and started again toward Sychar.

Another woman was walking in the same direction. Mara caught up with her. They exchanged greetings, then Mara asked, "In Sychar, do you know a woman called by the name of Nehushta?"

The woman stopped in surprise, glanced at her in scorn. Then she spat into the dust at her feet and quickly moved away.

The rejection was sharp, direct. But why? Mara felt stunned. What had she said to cause such a reaction? She'd asked a simple enough question. Was it her own speech? Were the dialects so different between Sebaste and Sychar people? Or was it the name Nehushta that had caused the reaction? She stepped around the spittle and walked on.

By the time she reached the village, the woman had vanished. Sychar's streets were deserted. Houses and buildings were indistinct masses in the dimness between the last of twilight and the start of moonrise. Here and there, a cookfire made a bright patch of orange light. But it would be the moon with which she would have to find her way.

Yet, even with light from such a heavenly orb, how could she find the house belonging to Cousin Nehushta? she asked herself. What should she do? How should she go about finding the right house? Or should she even bother to try, she asked herself, still thinking of the reaction of the village woman. She stopped in the middle of the street and once more questioned the wisdom of having come here. Feeling more alone than ever, she shifted the burden of her belongings to her other shoulder, walked to the side of the street, and sank wearily to the ground. Darkness closed in around her.

"I could die in this very spot," she said in a soft voice, glancing about. "And if I did, no one would know it, or care. I feel it in my bones."

"You, there!"

She glanced up, frightened. Two shapes loomed in front of her.

"Do you need help?"

It was a woman's voice, a not unkind one; and she could now recognize her shape. But the other shape was that of an animal, a very strange animal with two humps hanging off its sides. Mara scrambled to her feet, peering at it.

"Can I help you?" the woman asked, speaking again in common Greek.

Mara only made a stuttering sound, still peering at the animal until she gradually recognized it as a small donkey carrying two large waterskins on either side of its back. In spite of all, she giggled. "Your donkey frightened me for a moment," she explained. "He is a strange shape here in the dark with those two water-skins at his side."

The woman stepped around to see the animal as Mara did, and she, too, laughed.

Mara liked the sound of her laughter. It was light, friendly.

"Do you live here in Sychar?" the woman asked.

"No, I have come to see a relative. But in the darkness, I cannot find her house."

"Who is your relative?"

Wondering if she'd get the same response as from the first woman, she avoided answering directly. "My relative is a cousin. A cousin from my mother's family. She's lived here a long time. I haven't seen her in a long time. But I—I . . . I . . . I . . . "

"I've lived in Sychar for a long time, too." The woman's voice was patient. "I might know your cousin. What's her name?"

"Her name is Nehushta." Mara waited for a bad reaction, but none came. She felt better, liking this woman more and more. "Do you know Nehushta?"

"Yes, I know Nehushta."

"Then you know where her house is?"

"Yes."

"Then you will show me?"

"Of course, but . , . "

Uncertainty came over Mara again. "But what?"

"I think Nehushta may be away from her house. At least overnight. She even may be away from Sychar for a few days."

Mara's heart sank. Now what would she do? Where would she stay? Misfortune was with her harder than ever. She turned away to pick up her bundle of belongings.

"Where are you going?" the woman asked.

"I don't know."

"Do you know other people here in Sychar?"

"No. I know no one else in Sychar."

"Where will you stay?"

"I don't know."

"Then you must come and stay with me and my husband. And of course, with Dendo here." She gave the little donkey a gentle pat.

"Stay with you and your husband?"

"You must not sleep here in the streets. It wouldn't be safe for a young woman like you."

The moon had fully risen by this time, casting great brightness along the streets and deep blackness in the shadows of the houses and buildings. Mara now could see the woman's face. It looked as kindly as her voice had sounded. Great tears of relief and a curious new kind of joy welled up, stinging her eyes and giving vent to the awful pent-up emptiness she carried in her heart. "Thank you for your great hospitality."

"My name is Shua."

Mara smiled through the tears, thinking what a good name that was. It meant 'kindness.' What a good name, indeed.

"What is your name?"

"Mara." She wiped at her eyes with the back of her hand, wishing she had a cotton square like ladies used.

Shua provided one from the pocket of her tunic. "Come, Mara. It's only a little way to my house." She picked up the guide rope tied about the neck of the little donkey. It followed without hesitation as she moved down the street.

Mara picked up her burden of belongings and followed along, too.

Once they were inside the courtyard of Shua's house, an old man came to greet them and to lift the heavy waterskins from Dendo's back. Shua introduced him as Matri, her husband. He poured the water from the skins into large house pots and hung the skins on pegs to dry, relieving Shua of the chore.

The action surprised Mara. Her father would never have helped her mother in such a way. In fact, he wouldn't have helped her mother in any way with the household chores.

Matri closed and latched the courtyard gate, turned, smiled at Shua and led the way into the house.

Mara followed. The room was aglow with light from three tallow oil lamps; and it was larger than her parents' entire house. She took a quick breath in amazement and glanced at Shua and Matri with new appreciation. No one but rich people lived in a large house. Shua and Matri must be rich. And she was their guest. Had she finally eluded misfortune? Was good fortune to be hers at last?

Freshly cooked lentils filled the room with such a wonderful aroma that Mara's belly ached with new hunger.

Shua went to the firepit in the floor in which sat a large cooking pot. She picked up a big wooden ladle and stirred the lentils, then smiled up at Mara. "We will eat soon."

Mara nodded, thinking how much Shua's face reminded her of her mother's face. It was a face lined with age as her own mother's was; but there was a radiance and peacefulness in Shua's face that was different. Something else was different, too. Matri's face. His eyes held a gentleness she'd never seen before in any other man's eyes. And his thoughtfulness in helping Shua with the waterskins impressed Mara deeply.

"Who is your relative, Mara?" Matri asked after Shua explained why she was to be their guest.

"Her name is Nehushta."

The expression in the old man's eyes didn't particularly change, but he quickly cast a questioning look at Shua, who was filling a wooden bowl with lentils.

Mara wondered at the meaning of the look. Who was her cousin Nehushta? What was wrong with her? What did these strange reactions to her name mean?

"I thought it would be better to take Mara to Nehushta's tomorrow. During the daylight," Shua said quietly.

"I agree. It is the wise choice." Matri moved to the table at one side of the room, sat down and accepted the bowl of lentils Shua set before him. Instead of beginning to eat, Matri folded his hands in front of his chest and bowed his head.

Shua did the same thing.

Matri said in a reverential voice, "Lord God of us all, we thank You for our daily bread. Watch over us and our guest." He remained still with his head bowed for several moments, as if praying silently.

Shua did the same thing.

Mara watched, enchanted. Her father had never prayed before a meal. Her father and mother had never prayed at all, so far as she knew.

Matri lifted his head, unfolded his hands, broke off a piece of the coarse, brown bread on the table before him, and began to scoop up lentils from his bowl.

Shua returned to the firepit, filled two other bowls with lentils and bread chunks, and motioned for Mara to come and take one.

As she did, she asked, "Do you always pray like that before you eat?"

Shua nodded.

"Why?"

"The sacred scroll tells us we should, for it is the Lord God who provides all things for us."

Mara studied Shua's face carefully. She looked so sincere. She must really believe that everything was provided by the Lord God. But that idea puzzled Mara. She had wondered for some time if He provided for her, too. If He was the one responsible for providing her with all her misfortunes, then He was a god she was very unsure of. She sat down on the hard-packed earthen floor and began to eat. The lentils were tasty and hot. She ate ravenously. When she finished, she licked at her fingers and set the bowl on the floor beside her. She realized that Shua was watching her. Abruptly self-conscious, she smiled and wished that Shua would offer her another bowl of lentils.

Instead, Shua asked, "Have you come a long way in search of your cousin?"

Mara nodded, wondering if she dare ask for more lentils.

"Where do you come from?"

"From a place to the west of here," she said, unwilling to reveal too much about herself too soon. There was always the possibility that Matri and Shua might know Coniah.

Shua was patient. She ate for a bit, and then asked, "Do you have a family in the place where you come from?"

Mara shook her head, lying.

"We have no family, either. Except for each other," Shua explained in a forlorn tone. "It's just as well, I suppose, with all that my husband has to do in his position."

"What position is that?" Mara eyed the cooking pot still full of lentils.

"Why, Matri is town elder." Shua's face beamed with pride. "He has even been twice to Jerusalem. Once, he took me with him to pray in the women's court of the great Temple."

Mara widened her eyes. Being town elder meant that Matri gave advice and counsel to all who asked. It meant he could read and write. It meant he read the sacred scrolls and told the meaning of their words to people. It meant that Matri was not only rich, but important, too. Much more important than a gardener like her father. And it meant that Shua, as Matri's wife, was important too. And here she, a poor and unimportant stranger, was a guest in their house! Surely, good fortune was now smiling on her. At last. The idea emboldened her. She asked for more lentils.

Shua supplied them. "How long has it been since you saw your cousin?"

She finished eating and wiped her bowl clean with the rag of linen Shua handed to her. "It has been many years since I saw my cousin. I was just a child when she moved to Sychar. Have you known her a long time?"

"For some years."

"Since she came here?"

"I think so."

"What is she like?"

Shua stacked the last of the wooden bowls together and put them on a small table near the firepit. "She is an active woman."

"Is she a person of importance?"

"To some people, yes, she is important."

Matri stood up and walked out into the courtyard.

Shua went to the big table, picked up his bowl, wiped it clean and stacked it with the others. Then she went to the other side of the room and unfolded a stack of reed sleeping mats.

"What does my cousin look like?"

"Nehushta?"

"Yes."

"She has light-colored hair and light-colored eyes."

"Is she pretty?"

Shua turned, a sleeping mat in her hands, and motioned for Mara to place it beside the smoldering firepit. "It will be warmer for you there."

"Is she pretty?" Mara repeated.

"Who?"

"Nehushta." Mara grew curious at Shua's sudden distractedness. It was as if she really didn't want to talk about Nehushta any more than she herself wanted to talk about her own background. And again she wondered why.

"I'm sure she's pretty to some. But you will see, and judge for yourself tomorrow." Shua turned, took two other sleeping mats into her arms, and went into a small alcove. When she returned a moment later, she said goodnight and put out two of the tallow oil lamps. The third she left aflame.

Matri returned from the courtyard and went into the alcove. Shua followed.

Silence, deep and easy, broken only by the small sputterings of the tallow oil lamp, settled through the house. For Mara, sleep came quickly. In spite of her curiosity about Cousin Nehushta, and the reluctance of everyone to speak openly about her, she felt comfortable in the house of Matri and Shua.

Dawn came with the fresh promise of good fortune. Mara could sense it all around her. She had eaten well, slept well, and now with Shua she stood at the door of the house belonging to Cousin Nehushta. She rapped at the door. The excitement of anticipation went through her.

Her knocking brought no response. "Perhaps she has not returned after all," she said, glancing at Shua standing beside her.

"She is home," Shua's tone was surprisingly aggressive. She stepped forward and loudly rapped at the wooden door. "Nehushta! It is Shua. I have a surprise for you. Open your door."

There was a flicker of movement at the window.

Shua turned, patted Mara on the arm, and walked away toward her own house.

Mara shifted her bundle of belongings nervously from one arm to the other until the door finally swung open. Nehushta stepped out, curious, rubbing her eyes as if just awakened.

Disappointment shot through Mara. There was nothing familiar about the woman standing before her. Nothing matched her memories of childhood about this person. She remembered her as being taller and darker haired. And with a kindliness about her. But the woman staring curiously at her was short, almost white-haired, and her coarse-featured face held a hard, calculating look. There was a callousness about her that Mara was unprepared for. The familiar sense of misfortune fell over her again.

"Where is Shua?"

Mara could only point in the direction Shua had taken.

"And who are you?"

"I . . . I . . . I'm your cousin Mara. From Sebaste."

Nehushta's hard questioning look didn't change.

"My mother is Yasmin, wife of Hassad, and your first cousin on your mother's side."

"What do you want?"

"I have come to see you and visit for a while."

"Can you pay?"

"Pay? But I am your relative."

Two men passing along the street overheard, stopped, and called out. "No one stays with Nehushta unless they pay! Relative or stranger! Man or woman!"

Nehushta cursed at the men. They laughed and walked on down the street.

The full meaning of their remark came to Mara, and she could feel the flame of embarrassment rising in her face. Nehushta was a prostitute. Her own cousin Nehushta. A harlot.

With a dizzying sense of remembrance and comprehension, she now understood the village woman's reaction at the mention of Nehushta's name. She understood Shua's reluctance to show her Nehushta's house at night, or to talk about her. A harlot. Her cousin Nehushta, so lovingly remembered as a kind and good person, was a whore.

What was even worse, she now wondered if Shua and Matri thought that she, too, was a whore. The very idea set her trembling with anger and fear. She dropped the burden of her belongings. The stopper dislodged from the waterskin and its contents seeped out, soaking the shawl which protected her treasured doll. What could she do? What was to become of her? How could she ever change from being misfortune's pawn?

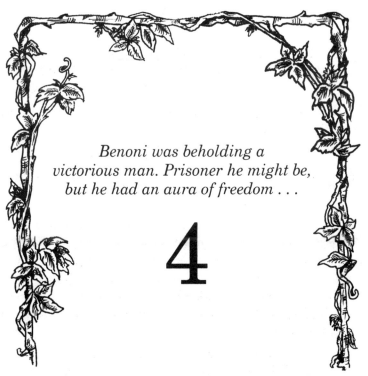

Benoni was beholding a victorious man. Prisoner he might be, but he had an aura of freedom ...

4

FOR BENONI, Machaerus was an astonishing sight. It looked for all the world like a large, cone-shaped mountain with its top cut off. It thrust upward thousands of feet from the briny flatness of the Dead Sea's eastern shore. Entrance was by a narrow road winding up around its perimeter.

Its history was as impressive as its size. At least that part of its history he had learned from both Roman and Jewish acquaintances. The great Jewish Hasmonean leader, Alexander Janneus, had originally fortified the site many years before. The Roman general Gabinius, under the command of Pompey, had destroyed it. When Herod the Great came to power during the reign of Caesar Augustus, he rebuilt the fortress and included a palace within it. Herod's son,

Herod Antipas, continued to maintain the mammoth structure as both fortress and palace.

Antipas regarded the site as strategically important, situated as it was above the south-to-north road from the Red Sea to Damascus. He also regarded it as a hideaway.

"And well it should be called a hideaway," Benoni said more to himself than to Rakem who had accompanied him on this unwelcomed journey. "Indeed, indeed. Machaerus is a hideaway. But what a hell-hole." He swiped at his forehead with a square of cotton fabric and loosened the leather thongs at the neck of his tunic. It didn't help much. The air was turgid here on the flats beside the Dead Sea. Turgid and stinking.

"Can you really see the fortress in this shimmering heat?" Rakem asked, shading his eyes.

Benoni pointed. "It's as big as the whole world! Of course I see it!"

Rakem rubbed at his eyes, fighting the glare of the midday sun, trying to find the outlines of the fortress against the redness of the mountains beyond. But to no avail. Instead, his glare-weary eyes fixed on a group of soldiers coming from a side trail in a great hurry. "What do you make of them, Benoni?"

Benoni shook his head, not ready to hazard a guess about anything. He had not wanted to come on this trip. Not at all. As Rakem had reported to him much earlier, Herod Antipas had, indeed, sent official notice to all of his scribes in all of his toparchies that they should assemble on this prescribed day at Machaerus for an accounting of numbers of travelers through their territories, who they were and what their business. And an accounting of any random reports of unrest, rioting, or political rabble-rousing.

Benoni found the summons ill-timed. It meant he had to hire someone to collect the road tax while he was away. And it also meant that he had to put aside his plans for a trip to Tiberias to see the Roman commander, Lucius Marcellus, about reinstating the road tax on the Perean road. The summons to come to Machaerus was very ill-timed.

Rakem pointed toward the oncoming squad of soldiers. "Something important must be happening. Why else would they hurry so in this god-forsaken heat?"

Benoni stopped, leaned on his walking staff, and watched. The soldiers were close enough now that he could see their faces shining with sweat under the close-fitting metal helmets. Their breastplates glinted in the sun, reflecting more heat up into their faces. Only the prisoner they pushed along inside their ranks seemed unaffected by the heat. He was a fierce-looking man with eyebrows thick and bushy above dark, deep-set eyes. His hair and beard were dark, uncut, matted and tangled, giving him the appearance of a wild creature. His clothing did nothing to relieve that impression. He wore an animal pelt with the fur still intact, a broad leather belt at his waist, and his feet were shod with a pair of well-worn leather sandals.

"Who is that?" Benoni asked. "A wild man from the desert?"

Rakem started to laugh, at the question, then caught himself and grabbed at Benoni's arm. "It's John!" he exclaimed in a stunned whisper. "It's John the Baptizer!"

"That's your prophet?" Benoni scoffed. "He's tethered hands and feet."

"Nevertheless, that's who it is." His hand tightened on Benoni's arm. "By all that's holy, my Jericho friends were more than right."

"What do you mean?"

"They told me that the Tetrarch was afraid of him. I didn't believe them." He pulled his hand away from Benoni's arm and cursed under his breath.

The squad of soldiers passed close by. Benoni now was able to see the prisoner very well. Not only was his appearance different from the normal garb most men wore, so was the look in his eyes. It was the kind of look that made Benoni doubt his own scoffing. It was a look of vision, of peace, of acceptance. In the Baptizer's eyes was a look of fulfillment rather than one of fear.

Benoni abruptly realized that he was beholding a victorious man, a man with an undaunted spirit. Prisoner he might be, but there was about him an aura of freedom that few prisoners had. It defied logic.

"Let's follow them," Rakem urged, wiping the sweat from his face.

Benoni needed no urging. He was already moving to follow the squad of soldiers up the narrow, winding roadway to the fortress-palace. All traffic coming down from the fortress made way for them.

The higher they climbed, the cooler it became. By the time they reached the top where the road widened at the sentry gate, a breeze was blowing. Benoni and Rakem both threw open their tunics as much as possible to catch the benefits of the breeze, and watched as the soldiers marched through the sentry gate without a pause. Benoni showed his papers to the sentry and they, too, passed through the gate into the great fortress.

It was market day at Machaerus. Brightly colored awnings and thatched shelters of a long line of booths cast welcome shade for the sellers of goods and for their customers. There was music, talking, laughter, vendors hawking their wares. The atmosphere was like that of a festival. The prisoner being hurried along in the midst of the soldiers seemed to be scarcely noticed.

Benoni stopped where a man was selling brooms. "Who is the prisoner with those soldiers?"

"He's called John the Baptizer."

"Why is he a prisoner?"

"It is said he offended the Tetrarch."

"See? I told you!" Rakem said.

"In all truth, though," the broom seller went on with a laugh, "it may be that it was the Tetrarch's lady he offended."

"The Tetrarch's lady?"

"Antipas's new wife, the Lady Herodias. She is reported to be quite angry because the prophet denounced her publicly for divorcing Philip to marry Antipas."

Rakem leaned close to Benoni. "I told you my friends in Jericho always have accurate information."

Benoni nodded distractedly, watching the squad of soldiers and their prisoner disappear through a wide arch in the palace wall. He turned again to the broom seller. "Where does the man John come from? What is his background?"

The merchant put aside the broom he was holding. "I hear he is from a priestly family. His father, a man named Zechariah, was a priest with duties at the Temple in Jerusalem. His mother, Elizabeth, is a cousin to the mother of the Galilean preacher."

"What Galilean preacher?"

"The one called Jesus of Nazareth."

Rakem tugged at his sleeve. "That is the Nazarene Matri and I were talking about just a day or two ago. Remember?" Benoni nodded again, wishing Rakem would quit interrupting.

The merchant straightened a stack of brooms. "Some people believe that John the Baptizer is the Jews' Messiah. But he denies it. He says someone else is coming who is greater than he. Some other people say that this Jesus of Nazareth is the Messiah."

"What do you think?"

The broom seller grew cautious. "Who can tell if anyone knows any truth about such things?"

Benoni thanked him and walked on, trying to piece together what he had just heard with what he already knew about the Jews and their laws. They had so many laws, it was hard to understand them sometimes. Samaritans didn't have quite so many laws. They were easier to understand. At least that's what he'd always thought. But now he was curious. If this John the Baptizer was of a priestly family, wasn't Herod Antipas risking trouble with the Jewish Sanhedrin by arresting him? He'd always heard that the priests with duties at the great Temple in Jerusalem had even more special privileges than any other priests. Arresting the son of such a priest made little sense. Maybe this wasn't John the Baptizer after all.

"Why so deep in thought, Benoni?" Rakem asked.

He told him what a puzzle this all was to him.

"Why, Benoni! I didn't think such a thing would bother you. I didn't think you cared about such things."

"Did you see the look in that man's eyes?"

"You mean the Baptizer?"

Benoni nodded.

"Why should you care?"

Benoni blushed, suddenly embarrassed at the realization that he had revealed some of his own deep inner feelings about a man he didn't even know. "You're mistaken, Rakem. I'm just curious."

But Rakem wouldn't let it go. "You do care. You care about what happens to that man. But why should you? Why should you care about some Jewish preacher who tells everyone to repent? You're not a Jew. Why should you care?"

Benoni stopped and looked squarely at Rakem. "The soldiers may have captured your John the Baptizer, but that man is no one's prisoner!"

Rakem's eyes widened with surprise. "The heat. That's it. The heat. It has gone to your head."

"Perhaps it has, my friend. But no matter. There is no need for us to argue. When I want to learn about religion, I will ask questions of someone like Matri, a man wise in the ways of religion and the laws. I'll not attempt to learn from someone like you."

Rakem's expression immediately changed to one of offense. "You think I know nothing!"

The reaction caught Benoni by surprise. He had not intended to offend his friend. He hurried to smooth it over by blustering and teasing. "That's right. You know nothing except about almost everything! But what you really know the best is about what we are surrounded by."

The blustering had good effect. Rakem looked confused. Benoni laughed and pointed to a booth just beyond Rakem's shoulder.

Rakem turned, saw the great mound of oranges from Jericho, and alongside them, cabs of Jericho's most famous product, balsam rum. He began to grin.

The merchant came forward, quoting prices, thinking he had a quick sale.

Rakem waved him off and turned again to Benoni. "Did you hear what they're charging for rum? Just think what we can charge with the supply we take back to Sychar."

Benoni laughed aloud. "It just might pay for this trip for both of us, eh?"

They walked on until they reached the wide arch through which the squad of soldiers and its prisoner had passed moments before. Two sentries now stood outside the arch.

Benoni stopped before one of them. "I am Benoni, Scribe of Sychar. The great Herod Antipas has summoned me. Do you know the place I should go?"

The sentry pointed through the archway to a wooden double door. "That is the entry to the Hall of the Scribes."

Benoni salaamed, as did Rakem, and together they made their way into the meeting place.

The meeting had already started. A scribe from one of the Judean toparchies was making his report to three men seated at a long table in the center of the room. It was hard to hear everything because of the murmur of talk and the shuffling about among the rest of the scribes.

"Is one of them Herod Antipas?" Rakem whispered.

Benoni shrugged. "I doubt that such an august personage as the Tetrarch would be in a meeting with regional scribes."

The man standing immediately in front of Benoni overheard them. He turned and said in a low tone, "You are right. The Tetrarch is not here. The man to the left is Manaen, his half-brother, and one of his close advisers. The man in the center is Chuza, Herod Antipas's steward of finances and household affairs. And on the right is Lucius Marcellus, the Roman commander at Tiberias."

The name Lucius Marcellus jumped at Benoni. He stiffened, astonished that he had not recognized him. But then, why should he? When the Roman had come to him for forged documents, he had never removed his helmet. Benoni stared at Lucius Marcellus, memorizing the look of him, scrutinizing every feature of his face: short cut hair combed forward, high cheek bones and aquiline nose, cloudy grey eyes under thin eyebrows, thin mouth that interrupted the bland, passive lower part of his face with a straight, hard line. That the Roman should be here in Machaerus was a pinnacle of coincidence. That he, Benoni, could be saved a trip to Tiberias was a most gracious gift of the gods. "By the gods," he whispered. "By the gods, indeed."

Rakem leaned close. "What troubles you?"

Benoni ignored him and bent forward to thank the man for identifying the officials at the table.

The Judean scribe completed his report. Chuza then began to question the scribe about John the Baptizer, and Benoni's interest was distracted from Lucius Marcellus.

"We hear this man of the wilderness is considered by many to be a prophet. And we also hear from many people that he claims to have baptized the Jews' Messiah. Do you know if this is true?"

At the mention of the word Messiah, the hall grew suddenly quiet.

"I, too, have heard the claim, Minister," the Judean scribe answered.

"Do you know if it is true?"

The man shook his head.

Chuza rose to his feet.

Benoni craned his neck to get a better view of him. He was a short, round man with a cherubic face and penetrating eyes. The physical appearance gave Benoni an odd sensation of kinship because of his own short stature and shape.

Chuza glanced about, searching the crowd. "If there is any among you who have first-hand knowledge of such a baptism, the Tetrarch would like to know about it. He would like to hear about it from you personally."

No one admitted having such knowledge.

"The Tetrarch would even reward the man possessing such knowledge," Chuza added.

The quietness only deepened.

"The reward would be large for anyone who has such first-hand information."

Still, all those gathered in the Hall of Scribes remained absolutely silent.

And suddenly, it dawned on Benoni that he had been right in the first place. All this interest in the baptizing of the Jew's Messiah had much more to do with political power than with any religious belief. He scrutinized the three officials. Each represented raw power. In differing ways, to be sure, but raw power, nevertheless. Herod Antipas's half-brother and close adviser on the left. A commander of an important Roman garrison on the right. And Chuza, the symbol and essence of Herod Antipas's own great power as the centerpiece of authority for and by the grace of Rome in Judea.

But what Benoni found of greatest interest was that they all apparently felt threatened by a rumor, a claim, that a wild looking, hermit-like preacher had baptized the Jew's Messiah. Why else would such powerful men waste their time on questions about a wilderness prophet?

Now he realized, too, why the capture and imprisonment of John the Baptizer was so important. Even though the reason given by the broom seller and by Rakem's friends held every possibility of truth, too, the factor of political power was something much more logical — something much more quickly understood.

And yet, there was still one thing Benoni could not logically understand. And that was the look he had seen in the eyes of the prisoner. If that prisoner was indeed John the Baptizer, then Herod's people and the Romans had a legitimate fear. Something beyond political power generated a look like the one he had seen in the prisoner's eyes.

But what could be beyond political power? Who was this Messiah? What was his power? How would it be manifested? Was it equally as powerful as politics with all its authority and wealth?

Chuza reseated himself, picked up a scroll and read from the list of scribes' names written thereon. One by one, the scribes responded to his questions about the numbers of travelers through their regions, and about unrest or agitation among the regions' citizens. Each time, his final question had to do in some way with either John the Baptizer or with the identity of the Jews' Messiah.

By the time his own turn came to report, Benoni had memorized the questions and his own answers to them. The north-to-south road carried more private citizens than the east-to-west road. More commercial and military travelers used the east-to-west road. No, he'd heard no talk about riots, even though many Galileans, who were notoriously independent and rebellious, traveled through his region.

Muffled laughter followed his comment about Galileans, and he observed that Lucius Marcellus seemed to be sitting rather more stiffly than before. He felt certain the Roman recognized him. He even considered the possibility of trying to talk to him here about reinitiating the roadtax in Perea. But almost in the same moment he decided against it. The timing was not right. He needed to go to Tiberias to discuss the tax situation.

His attention was brought back to the task at hand by a question put to him by Manaen. "What do you hear about a man named Jesus of Nazareth?"

Benoni hesitated, cautious of Manaen's tone of voice and trying to remember when he'd first heard of Jesus of Nazareth.

The hesitation caused Manaen some concern. "I asked you a question, scribe," he said impatiently.

"Apologies, honored sir. I was urging my poor memory."

"Well, what does your poor memory tell you?" Manaen urged.

"It tells me that I have only heard of the Nazarene once before today."

"And is your poor memory urged to tell us what you heard and where you heard it?"

Beside him, he sensed a sudden tenseness in Rakem, as if he were holding his breath. "No, honored sir, my memory is weak. Only once did I hear the name. It seemed unimportant. I know nothing of this Jesus of Nazareth."

Manaen was not satisfied. "We hear he is quite a preacher. We hear that he, too, like the Baptizer, preaches that a new kingdom is at hand."

Benoni shrugged.

"You've heard nothing like that in your region?"

Benoni shrugged again and turned his hands palms upward, pleading ignorance. "My region is full of Samaritans, honored sir. We have heard no one preaching about new kingdoms — or about old ones, either."

Again, muffled laughter came from the others. Close beside him, he sensed that Rakem's tenseness was subsiding. He could hear him breathe again.

"It is useless to press this scribe," Chuza said, interrupting Manaen. "The man obviously knows nothing of the Nazarene." Once more, he rose to his feet. "We thank all of you for coming, and for your reports. We encourage you to keep us informed on the matters discussed today. Also, the Tetrarch has asked me to extend the hospitality of his palace to you. Your housing is in the east wing. A dinner has been prepared for you there."

Manaen and Lucius Marcellus also rose to their feet and followed Chuza out of the hall.

"They have great interest in Jesus, haven't they?" Rakem said, coming up next to Benoni.

"So it seems. Perhaps we must find out more about him. He sounds politically important."

Rakem looked at him in a peculiar manner.

"Do you already know something more about him?"

"Only what you have already heard me discuss with Matri."

Benoni thought back to the conversation which had left him feeling so out of place.

"And of course," Rakem added, "there are many people who truly believe that Jesus could be the Jews' Messiah."

"Are you among them?"

Rakem avoided a direct answer. "Perhaps you should ask Matri about such an important religious answer."

Benoni grasped Rakem's arm. "I am asking you. Are you among those who believe this Jesus is the Jews' Messiah? And if you are, tell me why. It all sounds like such foolishness."

Rakem pulled free of his grasp. "Of course, my Greek friend, it all would sound like foolishness to you. There is no logic in such a miraculous possibility. And you are a man who believes only in logic. So how could you believe in the messiahship of Jesus?" He smiled enigmatically and walked back toward the huge doors through which they had entered.

Benoni slowly followed, feeling foolish as a schoolboy, and twice as perplexed at the sense of aloneness which once more overtook him.

"Get away from me. Get away from my house. Go and starve on someone else's doorstep!"

5

A FULL FOURTEEN DAYS had passed since Mara stood at Nehushta's door, stunned and disapproving of who and what her cousin was. Not knowing whether to flee or to wish to die on the spot, she had wailed to Nehushta. "What can I do? What will become of me?"

Nehushta pointed to the water-soaked shawl.

Mara gasped, realizing for the first time that she had dropped her bundle. She stooped, picked up the shawl and quickly unwrapped her treasured doll. It was not damaged. Only a little water had seeped through the shawl's heavy weave.

At the sight of the doll, a strange look crossed Nehushta's face. "I'll take you in. But you must pay."

"How can I pay? I have no money."

"And I can't support you. In some way, you must pay."

"But how—?"

"You will work for me."

Fear traced through her. "Work for you? Doing what?"

"Come inside," Nehushta ordered.

Mara brushed at the shawl in a futile attempt to dry it. "Why should I come inside?"

Nehushta glanced at her in surprise. "Because you have nowhere else to go. That is why."

"You have not told me what my work is to be."

"I have not decided."

"I will not come in your house until you do."

"Then leave! Get away from me. Get away from my house. Go and starve on someone else's doorstep." Nehushta spun into the house, slamming the door behind her. The wooden planks in the door shuddered. Angry bursts of dust rose from the threshold.

Mara began to tremble. Tears filled her eyes. Misfortune was everywhere. Now what could she do, she asked herself, realizing that she really had only three choices. She could become a beggar. She could kill herself and be done forever with all the aloneness and rejection. Or, she could work for Nehushta. Begging was out of the question. It was the one thing even lower than her own situation.

On the other hand, the idea of killing herself was not so easily put aside. She had thought of it every time

Coniah beat her. She even thought of it sometimes in quiet moments when she realized the futility of ever finding happiness. And always she thought of it whenever the unpredictable winds of misfortune scourged her hopes, as they now did. But even in those moments, she never thought beyond the idea of it; never considered how she might accomplish it; and in every instance, she had turned aside thoughts of the pain which she would have to endure in the doing of it. Until now.

Now, the idea of physical pain overwhelmed her. She had run from Coniah to avoid physical pain. Yet, if she tried to kill herself there was sure to be pain. She began to wonder if working for Nehushta would be less painful, even if the work Nehushta talked about meant giving herself to strange men.

And then a new worry came into her mind. Suppose Nehushta wouldn't take her in, after all? She had refused to enter the house. Suppose this stranger who was her cousin would not now allow her to enter?

But Nehushta did allow her to enter. In the ensuing fourteen days, she had come to realize that her disapproval of Nehushta meant nothing in the face of reality. Her own position was little better than that of a prostitute, for she was a married woman who had run away from her husband. In the eyes of customary law that put her at the mercy of all. She was in a strange village. She was alone. She had no skills, and no way to support herself. Except to work as a servant for her cousin.

Her duties were simple enough. In fact, they were duties she rather liked doing. She made certain that the fire in the fireplace never went out. She cooked, swept, dusted the beaded curtain which separated Nehushta's bed-chamber from the rest of the house, and fetched water from the well each twilight.

Nehushta had not yet ordered her to be with any of the men who came to the house. In fact, whenever a man came, Nehushta sent her away to wash clothes in the village's small stream just above the village in the foothills, or to buy fresh vegetables and fruits from the merchants in the marketplace, or to bake bread in the small courtyard at the back of the house. Sometimes when all the chores were done, and there was no place else for her to go, Nehushta sent her up onto the roof of the house to wait until the man left.

Mara was always glad to go, not wanting to hear the sounds that came from the alcove behind the beaded curtain, not liking the feeling of being an intruder or an unwanted observer. Lots of men came, day and night. She decided that Nehushta must be getting very rich. She wished she could find some way to get rich, and wondered what it would be like to give herself to strange men. At the very least, they would talk to her. That was something Nehushta never did, except to order her about. In this new life in which she had placed so much hope for friendship and understanding, she had found only the barest of tolerance. And she was still lonely.

She had not seen Shua, though she had gone twice to her house looking for her. Once on her way to wash clothes, she thought she saw Matri talking with a group of men near the city's eastern gate. Of all the women gathered at the washing place or drawing water at the well at twilight, only two had spoken to her. Her own response had been guarded. She feared trying to make friends, fearing they would turn against her as soon as they learned who her cousin was. She knew they would. She felt it in her bones.

She even wondered if she should take her doll and the shawl, a bit of food, and leave Sychar. But something deep in her spirit resisted that thought. Lonely as she might be, she had plenty of food and a warm place to sleep in Nehushta's house. And no one beat her. That was a new blessing. No one beat her.

On the fifteenth day a cold rain came out of the northwest, drenching the village of Sychar and reducing all activities to a minimum. "It is a bad omen," Nehushta said, opening the door a bit and peering out at the wet street empty of traffic. "There will be no money made this day."

"It will be good for you to rest a day," Mara said, stirring at a pot of lentils and wondering why they didn't smell as good as those she'd had at Shua's house.

Nehushta closed the door and looked around at her with a peculiar expression. "You mean it will be good that you won't have to get out in this rain, don't you?"

Mara didn't answer, but sipped at the lentils, testing them. They didn't taste as good as Shua's. Shua must have used some different herbs or spices in her lentils, Mara decided. Or maybe she had been so hungry that first night in Sychar that her imagination had made her believe Shua's lentils smelled and tasted so good. Or maybe they tasted better because she had been made to feel welcome in the house of Shua and Matri. She certainly felt no welcome here.

Nehushta came toward her. "Doesn't it worry you that if I make no money, you don't eat?"

"What, my cousin?"

"Doesn't it worry you that you might not get fed?"

Mara put down the wooden ladle. "I have friends who will feed me, if you don't." The response popped out unexpectedly. Surprised at her own boldness, she glanced quickly away, not daring to look at Nehushta.

"You have a quick tongue."

Mara blushed.

"Do you care so little for my kindness?"

It was the first time Nehushta had spoken to her other than to give orders. And something about her tone reminded her of childhood squabbles with Timna. Timna would always start an argument with a question that couldn't be answered without an argument. Suddenly, Mara felt challenged to defeat Nehushta with words.

"Do you care so little for my kindness?" Nehushta asked again.

"I work for what you feed me."

"What did you say?"

"I said I work for what you feed me."

"Ingrate!"

"Ingrate? Who else would do for you what I am doing without pay?"

A frown creased the space between Nehushta's eyes. "You eat more than you earn."

"That is your opinion."

"That is my knowledge."

"Very well! Then, I shall do as the wise men say it is written to do."

"And what might that be?"

"Better it is to dwell in a corner of the housetop than with a brawling woman in a wide house."

Anger streaked Nehushta's face. She stood up.

Mara stood up too, and fully expecting to be hit, braced herself.

But the blow came in words. "If I am too much of a brawling woman for you, then do as the men of wisdom say." She pointed to the door. "Get yourself out and up onto the rooftop."

Mara's feeling of challenge evaporated. The rain continued its cold, steady downpour beyond the door. "The rooftop? But—it's pouring rain . . . "

"The men of wisdom should have thought of that! Go, I say. Out!"

Mara went to her reed sleeping mat and picked up her doll and shawl. She tucked the doll carefully inside her tunic, and threw the shawl over her head and shoulders.

Nehushta snatched the shawl from her. "This is no longer yours. I take it back!"

Nehushta's action was so quick that it stunned her. She stood staring in disbelief, and let herself be pushed out of the house. The cold rain hit her face, forcing the fog of astonishment from her head.

She pulled her tunic closer around her to protect the doll, and looked about. The streets were empty. No person and no animal could be seen. Even the village dogs had taken refuge somewhere. What a fool she was. And what could the wise men have been thinking of to write down such a guidance about a brawling woman?

She turned and ran for the house of Shua and Matri. The gate to the courtyard was already open. She went in. In spite of the rain, the door to the house was open. She paused at the open doorway and rapped as loudly as she could on the doorpost.

Within a few moments, Shua appeared, recognized her and began to smile. She held out her arms in a beckoning gesture.

Mara stepped into the house, accepting the embrace of friendship with such an unaccustomed sense of belonging that tears welled up inside her once more. She fought to hold them back, lest they spoil a rare moment of joy.

"We have been worried about you."

"I came to see you twice. But, you were away."

Shua held her at arm's length, studying her face. "Nehushta is being kind?"

Mara nodded. "She has fed me, given me a servant's work." She hesitated, ashamed to confess that she had caused her own dismissal from Nehushta's house.

Shua misread the hesitation and frowned. "And what other work did she give you?"

"You mean with the men? None."

A relieved look overtook Shua's frown. "It is good."

"But I have made Nehushta angry," Mara finally confessed. "She told me to leave. In fact, she shoved me out!"

"All the better. Now, there will be no obligation for you to return to her. Your obligation to your blood relative is paid."

"What do you mean?"

"You, as a traveler, sought her, your relative, for shelter first," Shua explained. "Now, she has thrown you out. There is no obligation for you to return to her. It is the custom, my child, a very old and traditional custom."

Matri came in from a room at the rear of the house which Mara had not noticed during her previous visit. He was followed by two other men. One of them was fairly tall and lean. The other was short and plump. She decided at once that the short, plump man was the more important. Suspended from his neck on a leather cord was a large, official-looking signet ring.

Matri greeted her in friendly fashion. "Mara, these are our friends Rakem and Benoni."

She nodded and lowered her eyes in the custom of politeness she had been taught as a child.

"Mara is a new friend," Shua explained, coming to stand beside her. "She has only recently come to Sychar to find a relative. Unfortunately, the relative has moved away."

Shua's lie surprised her until she saw the look of quick understanding between Shua and Matri, as if they had suspected all along that Nehushta would throw her out.

The short, plump man seemed to notice the reaction, too, and he looked at her with interest.

"We expect that Mara will stay with us until she can make new plans," Shua went on.

"Then, we shall see her again," Rakem grinned. "That will be a pleasure, eh, Benoni?"

Benoni smiled.

She blushed, unaccustomed to approval from men.

"Come, Mara," Shua said. "Will you help me with the baking of bread?"

She nodded, grateful for a way to escape from the approval of both men. But particularly from Benoni's interest. For he looked at her in a way that made her feel self-conscious, and strangely uncomfortable. She liked the idea of their approval, but she didn't fully trust it. She scurried after Shua, who was disappearing into the sheltered area of the courtyard.

"What do you know about her?" Benoni asked, turning to Matri.

The old man shook his head. "Not a great deal. Shua found her in the streets a few nights ago."

"Who is her relative?" Rakem asked. "I can think of no one who has moved away from Sychar in recent times."

"You are right, my friend. No one has moved away."

"Except for those who've died," Benoni said.

Rakem ignored him. "But, Shua said — "

"What my good wife said was to save the girl's pride."

"But why . . . ?"

"Who, in the entire village, would you least like to have as a relative?" Matri asked. "Who, in the entire village, would bring shame to you, if you were a relative?"

Benoni stiffened, and said in a low tone of astonishment, "Nehushta?"

Matri nodded.

Rakem's eyes widened. "That innocent-looking thing is a relative to Nehushta?"

"They are cousins. On the girl's mother's side of the family. At least, that's what she told Shua."

"Women, and their relatives," Rakem's voice held a sorrowful tone.

"Where is she from?" Benoni asked.

Matri shook his head. "She was careful to tell Shua very little about herself. She acted frightened."

"She could be a runaway slave," Rakem suggested.

"Or a runaway wife," Benoni added, fingering the signet on its leather cord.

Both men looked at him in surprise.

"Why do you say that?" Rakem wanted to know.

Matri chuckled. "Because he wants a woman of his own."

Benoni swung around on the stool, stood up, went to the door. It was still raining. Not as hard as before, but hard enough that the raindrops beaded together on the edge of the thatched shelter and created a fringe of liquid crystals. He looked out at Mara and Shua busy grinding the barley for the bread. Neither of them hesitated in their work or looked up at him. Yet, he had the feeling they had been talking and suddenly stopped when he appeared at the doorway. He wondered if they were talking about him.

If she can bake bread, she can cook, he thought. And she most likely can clean a house and keep it in order. Then he wondered how good she would be as his woman. She was pretty in a shy sort of way, not too tall for him. He liked her long, dark hair, and her soft, dark eyes.

She glanced up at him, and blushed.

Shua noticed, and stopped her work. "You are welcome to stay and break bread with us, Benoni. You and Rakem both. Mara and I are baking extra bread. And there will be a pot of stew with lamb in it."

"Your kindness is softer than a raindrop in the spring, and twice as welcome."

Shua arched one eyebrow. "I take that to mean you accept the invitation."

He grinned, winked at her, and went back into the main part of the house.

As he disappeared, Mara turned to Shua. "Tell me about him. What is this Benoni like?"

"He is Herod's scribe. Do you like him?"

"He is an important man, isn't he?"

Shua nodded. "Next to Matri, he is the most important man in Sychar."

"Is he rich?"

A gentle smile came over Shua's face. "No, my child. He is not rich. But neither does he live in poverty.

I think he is clever about always having enough shekels."

"Then, as Herod's scribe, he is paid well?"

"I suppose he is paid as well as anyone who works for the Tetrarch. But, there may be other ways that Benoni adds to his earnings," she said.

Mara studied the older woman, wondering exactly what she meant, hoping it was nothing bad, like Nehushta. Then, on second thought, she knew that Benoni would not be welcome in the house of Shua and Matri if he were a bad person.

All during the meal, Mara watched him from her place beside Shua near the firepit. She tried to be careful so he would not know she was watching him. But once or twice he glanced up so quickly to look at her that she had no time to look away, and their eyes met and held for the merest moment. Mara found it not unpleasant.

During the next several days, she saw no more of him. Nor of his friend, Rakem. But she thought of him often; wondered where he was and what he was doing; considered whether or not she had imagined his interest in her. She started several times to ask Shua, but feared that to do so would arouse too much of the older woman's curiosity.

She contented herself with the tasks that filled each of her days now as a member of the house of Shua and Matri. In addition to the normal everyday tasks, she helped Shua fix extra food for sick neighbors. She ground barley or rye for the baking of bread, and even helped with the kneading of it sometimes. She started learning to weave small squares and strips of cotton and linen, which were used for all sorts of purposes. Shua sold some of them as face veils. Others were sold as headbands. Many village women liked to wear them when they were inside their houses rather than wearing the longer, heavier head shawls.

But the task she enjoyed the most was going to the great well late each afternoon with Shua and the little donkey, Dendo. Every woman in the village knew Shua and respected her. Shua introduced her as her friend and house guest.

The women all seemed to accept her. She liked their acceptance, enjoyed being a part of the village, listened carefully to the village gossips. The widow Hodesh was usually the person with the most news. Shua called her the town gossip, and warned Mara to be cautious of her.

One afternoon on the way to the well, Mara finally asked Shua about Benoni. "Is he away from Sychar?"

"He and Rakem went to Tiberias the day after you met him. When the rain finally stopped," Shua told her. "Benoni has business there with the Roman commander. He has been there twice since coming back from Machaerus. And sometimes, he and Rakem go on to a place on the River Jordan to fetch papyrus for scrolls."

"Doesn't Herod supply his scribes with scrolls?"

Shua shrugged. "Benoni has use for many scrolls. Some for his own business."

"His own business? What kind of business?"

Shua patted her arm and changed the subject. "Benoni takes Rakem with him because he is both good company and a help in gathering papyrus."

She asked no more questions, knowing it would be useless to do so. Shua would be as clever about not explaining all she knew about Benoni's business as she had been about not explaining all she knew about Nehushta. She had not seen her, either, since the day she had been thrown out of the house.

In the back of her mind, she had expected to see Nehushta sometimes at the well. But she hadn't. It was as if her cousin simply did not exist in the life of the village of Sychar. She had never even heard the widow Hodesh mention her. For such a small village, that seemed most strange.

Then one day, Shua asked her to go alone to fetch the water. "Matri has another task for me," Shua explained. "There is no reason why you should not fetch the water by yourself. Take Dendo with you to carry it."

Mara did as she was asked. Several of the women from the village were already at the well, and they greeted her kindly as she joined them.

The widow Hodesh came toward her. "Where is Shua? She is not ill, I hope."

"No, she is not ill. She was busy with other chores and asked me to fetch the water for her."

"Do you like living in the house of Shua and Matri?" Hodesh inquired.

"Yes." Mara said, moving away to take her turn at the well. She lowered the leather bucket into the well, felt it fill with water, retrieved it and filled first one jug and then another. The little donkey stood quite still with practiced patience until Mara completed the task.

"Fancy, my, how fancy!"

At the sound of Nehushta's voice, Mara swung around.

An awful silence settled over the other women. It was plain to see their disapproval and their dislike of Nehushta. It was also plain to see their curiosity about how she and Nehushta knew each other.

Nehushta came toward her. "When you first came to this village, you had only a waterskin made from the stomach of a goat. Now look at you! You have a donkey, two household jugs and a leather bucket with which to draw from this great well."

"What do you know of this person, Mara?" Hodesh asked.

Mara felt paralyzed.

Nehushta ignored Hodesh's intrusion. "Your waterskin is still in my house, Mara."

"What would a child such as this be doing in your house, Nehushta?" Hodesh demanded.

"What, indeed?" asked another woman from the edge of the crowd.

"You're a troublemaker, Nehushta," Hodesh charged. "This child knows nothing of you. And knows nothing of your house."

"Oh yes, this child, as you call her, knows me very well," Nehushta laughed. "She is a cousin to me!"

The women all gasped in surprise.

A look of disbelief crossed the face of the widow Hodesh. "This cannot be true!"

Nehushta laughed again. "Oh, it is true! And it matters very little that Shua is protecting her. She will still have to come back to my house when I say so."

"For what reason?" Hodesh demanded.

"She works for me!"

The women all looked at Mara, expecting her to defend herself. But so strong was her fear that she could find no words.

The women began drifting away. One by one they headed back for the village until only Hodesh remained, staring hard at Nehushta as if that action alone would be enough defense.

But Nehushta defiantly stared back, an insolent curve at the corner of her mouth.

Mara felt sick inside. She clutched at the rope around Dendo's neck, knowing she should leave. And quickly. Twilight was dwindling. Shua would begin to worry. But she knew, too, that she could not leave the widow Hodesh to fight her battle. Why had Nehushta done this? Why? After so many days of silence, why had she done this?

So tightly was her attention focused on Hodesh and Nehushta that she did not hear the footsteps coming toward them from the far side of the well. In fact, it was not until Benoni and Rakem were standing right beside her that she knew they were there. She gasped, startled, yet strangely relieved.

Benoni stepped past her into Nehushta's line of sight.

Nehushta glanced toward him, hate glinting in her eyes.

"Begone, woman of the streets," Benoni ordered. "Leave decent women in peace."

"What decent women? The town gossip? And an ingrate brat of a cousin?"

With surprising speed, he stepped toward Nehushta, menacing.

She spat at him.

He ignored it, grabbed her arm and twisted it. "Begone, I said. You have no claim on Mara. Bother her again, and I'll have the Romans put you in prison."

She laughed sneeringly. "The Romans will never do it. They still come to me, even if you don't!"

"They'll do whatever I ask them to do. Now begone, you piece of brass!"

"You will regret this, tax-collector," she threatened. "Make no mistake. And so will you regret it, Mara. So will you!"

*From a shielded spot
beside the stream, he watched her bathe.
She knew he was there.*

6

"RAKEM, FOLLOW NEHUSHTA," Benoni ordered. "We'll need to know what mischief she plans for us."

Without hesitation, Rakem departed.

Benoni came back to Mara. "Did she harm you?"

Mara shook her head. It had all happened so quickly; her tongue still could find no words.

"Mara is wrong," Hodesh spoke up. "Nehushta has done her harm. Every woman in the village knows of their blood kinship, and that Mara worked for her."

"But Mara is no harlot. That is not the work she did in Nehushta's house!"

Hodesh shook her head. "It makes no difference. The women who were here will tell all their neighbors. The news will spread like fire blown by a gusty wind. The women will not forget. Mara has been harmed."

"But Mara is no harlot, I tell you!"

"The women will always wonder. And they'll make life in this village miserable for Mara."

"Then, the women are as silly as geese!" His tone of disgust was complete. He turned to Mara and gently urged, "Take Dendo back to Shua and Matri. Hodesh will go with you."

The moment they arrived at Matri's house, Hodesh blurted out every detail of what had happened at the well. And with her every word, a fearful sadness grew in Mara's heart. These past few weeks had been the happiest she could remember. Now, the happy times were about to be taken away from her. Could she never escape the grasp of misfortune? Was it always to be her fate to be unlucky?

She looked at Matri and Shua. Their faces were stern, disapproving of what Hodesh was telling them. Was the brief happiness she'd known with them to be lost? Would they ask her to leave their house? She could not blame them if they did. But where would she go? What could she do? She walked to the firepit, sat down near it, pulled her knees up to her chest and sadly rocked back and forth while Hodesh finished telling what had happened at the well.

To Mara's surprise, it was Matri who reacted first. He came to her, placed his hand on her head. "We will protect you, my child." He turned and went out into the courtyard where she could hear him talking to someone else. Shua heard it, too, and went to the door to see who it was. "Benoni and Rakem have come," she said, returning. "Mara, help me put food out for them. They will be hungry after their long journey from Tiberias."

Mara got up at once to help. By the time the men came into the house, bread, cheese, bowls of lentils and cups of rum had been placed on the table, and she and Shua joined Hodesh near the firepit.

The men ate in silence. Mara wondered if it was because Hodesh was still there. When they finished eating, they went into the inner room. Only a murmur of their voices could be heard, except for one instance when Benoni's voice grew loud and angry as he mentioned Nehushta's name. It was obvious they were discussing what should be done in retaliation. Mara also realized that her own fate was being discussed, and she wondered again what was to become of her.

Hodesh got up to leave.

"Our thanks to you for standing by Mara against Nehushta," Shua said, going with her.

Hodesh shrugged, pulled her shawl close about her and went across the courtyard and out the gate. Shua latched the gate behind her and returned to the house.

Matri led Benoni and Rakem back into the main room where they all sat down again at the table. "We have been discussing how we can best protect you, Mara," he said, stroking his beard and staring at the hard-packed earthen floor.

"And we think we know a way to do it," Rakem added.

She glanced from one to the other, fearing the worst.

Matri folded his arms in front of his chest and studied her for a moment. "Benoni needs someone to cook, clean, and do other chores for him. For the work done, he will house, feed and clothe that person."

"But, that person must be a woman I can trust," Benoni said, looking at her squarely. "Would you be such a woman, Mara?"

Had she heard him right? Could she really believe her ears? This important man was asking her to work for him in his house? This important man was trusting her enough to even ask? She looked at Shua and Matri. But their expressions were passive.

She turned, searching Benoni's face. He seemed sincere. But had he already forgotten what misfortune she brought on people who befriended her? Had he already forgotten how he had to rescue her from Nehushta?

She paced away, her heart pounding with the hope of his offer. It would be—

Abruptly, she stopped, remembering that she was still married to Coniah. How would that affect this offer? she wondered, her spirits sinking. No one in the room knew about Coniah. She had never told anyone about him.

"Say yes to Benoni, Mara," Rakem grinned at her. "Tell him yes, or I shall have to do all those womanly chores for him!"

Matri chuckled, then quickly grew serious again. "Benoni can protect you, Mara, if you are his housekeeper. He is a very important man in this village. You will be safer with him than with anyone else in Sychar."

She hesitated, her conscience torn between wanting to say yes, and not wanting to tell them she was married. What would happen if she did tell them? Without asking, she knew the answer. Benoni would find some other woman to do his chores. She knew it in her bones. On the other hand, why should she worry about whether or not they knew she was a married woman? Benoni was only asking her to work for him. He was not asking her to marry him. Why should she worry about Coniah? Why shouldn't she say yes?

Why shouldn't she, indeed! Slowly, she turned to Benoni, and lowering her eyes in a gesture of courtesy, said, "I thank you, sir. I should like to be a woman you can trust."

"As it is said, so shall it be done," Benoni said, smiling at her.

Shua came to her and embraced her.

Matri nodded approval.

Rakem grinned again at her.

"This very night," Benoni said, "I shall begin a search for a new and larger house. I have been thinking of doing that, anyway. Now, I definitely shall. Come, Rakem, help me search."

The new house Benoni purchased was situated only a short distance to the east of Matri's. It, too, had a gated courtyard, a sleeping alcove off the main room, and an inner room. There were differences, though. The inner room of Benoni's house had a trapdoor in one corner of the ceiling, and a ladder positioned beneath it which could be used to climb to the roof of the house.

Ordinarily, Mara wouldn't have given a second thought to a ladder to a roof. Every house in every village had a ladder allowing access to its rooftop from its courtyard. But this ladder was inside the house, and out of sight. Almost as if it were a secret. Across from it, and concealed with a large animal skin, was a door which led outside to a short street that separated the back of Benoni's house from the city's wall.

It was an odd arrangement, too. From Mara's first day in the new house, she wondered about it. When she asked Benoni, he dismissed it by saying the previous owner had put the doorway there, and that it was seldom used. The answer did not satisfy her curiosity. She continued to wonder about it, especially whenever she saw fresh footprints in the dust of the packed earth floor.

Fresh footprints were there often. Benoni had many visitors. Many of them were taxpayers who came through the courtyard. But many others came and went through the inner room. She knew some of the footprints belonged to Rakem. He came and went frequently, and at all hours. He was not only a friend to Benoni, but worked at various jobs for him, too. Since he could read and write almost as well as Benoni, he was of great assistance. Reading and writing was something she would like to be able to do someday. If good fortune continued to smile on her, maybe that, too, would happen.

In the meantime, she discovered that being Benoni's housekeeper had unexpected benefits. At Matri's house, she had been a guest. And though she helped Shua with the chores, it was as a guest and as a new friend. There was a temporary quality and a sense of impermanence about it all. Just as there had been at Nehushta's — though for quite different reasons.

But here in Benoni's house, she knew her place, knew what was expected of her, and felt a sense of permanence about it. She was a housekeeper in the full sense. She cooked, cleaned, baked bread, mended Benoni's clothes, and arranged papyrus scrolls in neat stacks in the inner room for him.

He taught her how to carefully store charcoal sticks in small clay pots near his writing table in the main room of the house; how to cut styluses from the stiff ends of papyrus reeds; and he promised to teach her how to prepare scrolls from papyrus.

She also fetched their needed supply of water each day from the great well. But she never went there alone. Benoni was quite strict about that. He allowed her to go only when Shua went.

With Shua at her side, no one bothered her. Neither did any of the other women speak to her. They talked around her. It was as if they could not see her, as if she didn't exist. She wished this were different, but since it wasn't, she made the best of the situation.

Making the best of situations was beginning to seem less and less hard to do. Too many other things in her life were new and interesting. Though Benoni was a stern taskmaster and expected much of her, he was kind. He respected her feelings about her shawl and her beloved doll, and gave her a special shelf for them in the inner room. He asked Shua to make two new tunics for her; and he himself bought a wonderful Galilean homespun robe for her from a merchant who came to the house to pay his travel taxes.

But the change she liked more than all the rest was that Benoni talked to her. Nearly every night after he had eaten, he would pull his sleeping mat from the corner of the room, place it near her own at the firepit, settle onto it and talk to her. Sometimes, he talked about things she didn't really understand; things like politics and religion, and the Romans and money, and documents that needed to be altered or corrected. She listened carefully, wanting to know more about the things that interested him. And more than that, wanting to know more about him. Shua had told her where he had come from, and about the importance of his work as Herod's scribe. But now that she lived in his house, was his servant, she wanted to know more about him as a person. She wondered about things that only he could tell her about himself, for she was becoming more and more attracted to him.

Short and round as he was, his surprising agility never ceased to astonish her. He had a grace of movement like none of her husbands. He was clean. Sometimes he bathed twice in as many days, something none of her husbands had done. To show him how much she liked his cleanliness, she began to bathe more often herself by going in the very early mornings to a hidden place on the small stream that ran beside the village.

It was on one of these early mornings that she was startled to see Benoni walking along the stream's bank while she bathed. Quickly she reached for her garment and pulled it around her shoulders, her heart pounding in embarrassment that he might have seen her unclothed.

"Good morning," Benoni called as he approached. "I am sorry . . . I did not mean to startle you."

He paused at the stream's edge. From his demeanor Mara could not tell whether Benoni had deliberately followed her or if their meeting was accidental. She swept her wet hair back with both hands, then gathered her garments about her as she rose.

"I was bathing," she apologized, "but I am finished now."

"You are beautiful," Benoni said.

With the flush of embarassment still lingering in her heart, she could not look him in the eyes. Did he truly think she was beautiful?

He reached out and took her hand as she climbed toward him. Then he took both hands in his and drew her close.

"Look at me, Mara."

Slowly, hesitantly, she lifted her gaze until her eyes met his.

"I will take you for my woman."

Mara's heart was flooded with conflicting emotions. Though it was not considered improper for a master to lie with his servant girl, something told her that making love with Benoni was not right—not yet. Yet his gentle embrace was so different—there was no harshness, no coercion or violence.

He led her toward a thicket of bushes along the stream, then paused to kiss her in a full embrace. Just then she heard the snap of a reed and footsteps running away. Benoni heard it too. They both turned, startled and wary, in time to see the retreating figure of Hodesh disappear in the direction of the village.

The villagers' reactions to Hodesh's report varied.

"So Herod's man finally has his own woman," one neighbor laughed. "In his happiness, let's pray for smaller taxes!"

The cheesemaker said, "Maybe now he'll pay a decent price for my cheeses."

"Benoni always tried to cheat me," Nehushta cursed when told about the incident. "Good riddance."

"It was bound to happen," Rakem told Matri.

"I expected it to happen sooner," Matri replied.

But Shua's reaction was less lenient. She predicted retribution. "Without benefit of wedding vows, living together is a sin. The sacred scroll is very clear on that matter. They will both pay for it."

"She is but a servant, Benoni the master," Matri contradicted. "It is his right to lie with her if he wishes. It is within the law of man."

Shua was adamant. "It is not within the law of God. They will both pay for it."

And Shua's prediction was accurate. Retribution came quickly. That very night, in fact, when she once again took Mara to the well with her, the women of the village made it plain they would have nothing to do with Mara. Before, they simply had ignored her, but on this night they were loud and cutting. Their protest was one of outrage.

"You are a true cousin to Nehushta!"

"Brass."

"Foul!"

"Woman of the streets."

"Abomination!"

"Harlot!"

"Nehushta sells herself for money. What do you sell yourself for?"

"Get out of Sychar!"

With every outcry, tempers rose, until a throng of women shoved Shua aside and set upon Mara, attacked her, hit at her with their waterbuckets.

Mara fled, sickened by the anger of the throng, panicked by the violence, terrorized by the prospect of once more being alone, of being an outcast.

She burst into Benoni's house, pale and shaken. He had a visitor, a Roman soldier. In spite of being on the verge of hysteria, she realized that they had been quarreling. But whatever their argument, they stopped in surprise at her entry. She turned abruptly to go back into the courtyard.

Benoni followed her. "What has happened?"

She described the scene at the well.

A strange, twisted expression crossed his face. Anger glinted in his eyes. "Was Nehushta there?"

"I didn't see her."

"Do you know the names of the women who attacked you? Or the names of their husbands?"

She shook her head.

Villagers, curious and prying, began to gather in the street in front of the house and peered through the open gate.

The Roman soldier came and stood in the doorway of the house, looking out. "If she was my woman, I'd take—"

"But she isn't your woman!" Benoni cut him off, going to the gate and closing it. "Wait here until I finish my business with this Roman," he ordered Mara and went back into the house, shoving the Roman in front of him, and resuming their argument.

Their words came in such rapid anger that Mara could understand only a few of them. But the argument seemed to be about the price Benoni wanted to charge for some documents.

Outside in the street, the voices of the villagers grew louder and louder, until she could no longer hear Benoni and the Roman.

Trembling with fear, she sank down into a corner of the courtyard, hid her face in her hands, and began to sob. Misfortune once more clutched at her; grabbed from her the small bits of happiness she had found. And what of the Roman soldier still arguing with Benoni inside the house? Was her own misfortune now wrapping its awful tentacles around Benoni, too? Would there never be a finish to it? How many ways were left in which misfortune could hurt and frighten her?

The outcry from the people in the streets increased; overlaid now by added high-pitched indignation of the village women who had been at the well. Then, punctuating the awful din, came the thudding sounds of stones being hurled against the gate and the wall of the courtyard.

"Bring forth your harlot, scribe," shouted a man near the gate.

"Death to the harlot!" shouted another.

The stones were meant for her! The stoning was meant for her as surely as they would have been for a common woman of the streets. Fresh new fear swept over her. She clapped her hands over her ears, trying to shut out the dreadful accusation, and cringed against the dusty ground of the courtyard.

"Come, Mara, come with me!" Rakem's voice, abruptly close by her, overrode the shouting throng now pounding at the gate. Rakem lifted her to her feet and ran with her into the house.

The main room was empty. Benoni and the Roman were gone. Her heart sank. Benoni had deserted her! He was no better than any other man she'd ever known. She'd been a fool to ever think otherwise.

"Come quickly," Rakem urged, pulling her toward the inner room. "We must get you out of here to safety."

"But where?"

"Matri's house. Come quickly, through the rear door."

She pulled back, halting him. "My doll, my shawl! I must take them with me!"

"Leave them. You'll be back." He jerked her forward, shoved aside the animal skin hiding the rear door, pushed her through it, and led her carefully, silently, through the winding back streets of Sychar to the safety of Matri's house. Within moments of their arrival, a new sound came to her from the streets. It was the hurrying tramp of heavy boots.

"The Romans! Benoni found them!" Rakem said, a tone of relief clearly in his voice.

Mara looked at him in astonishment. "The Romans? Benoni went after the Romans?"

"Of course. Where did you think he went?"

She did not answer.

Rakem looked at her closely. "Silly goose, don't you know that civil disorder is the thing Romans fear the most in this land?"

"But Benoni was arguing with that Roman in the house . . . "

"True. But when the mob began to stone the gate, they quit arguing and went to get reinforcements from the camp beyond Mount Gerizim."

"And I thought . . . "

"What did you think, Mara?"

Shua came to her. "Did you think that Benoni had deserted you?"

"What else was I to think?"

"Benoni may be many things, my child. But he is no coward, nor will he abandon his friends." Shua touched her shoulder. "It is a new thing for you to know a man who will respect a woman. Especially a woman servant. But Benoni is such a man."

"But the villagers . . . they called me a . . . "

"We know what they called you. It does not matter," Rakem said.

"You are but a servant," Matri spoke up from the far side of the room. "If, as master, Benoni wishes to have his way with you, you cannot stop him."

"Then why such an outcry against me?" Mara demanded.

"Because of Nehushta." said Matri. "Benoni has levied a new tax on her. Or rather, on the services she renders."

"It is a very unpopular tax," Rakem said with a grim laugh. "It is as unpopular with the men of the village as it is with Nehushta."

Shua interrupted. "Nehushta was furious that Benoni took you as his servant, Mara."

"But Hodesh was the one who—"

"I know, I know," Shua went on. "Hodesh is a foolish old tongue-wagger. She has told many untrue tales to Nehushta about you these past few weeks. She intended to upset Nehushta, to feed her jealousy, to laugh at her. And, when she saw you and Benoni together near the stream, she couldn't wait to spread the news that you have been lovers since the first night you entered Benoni's house."

"But that's not true!" Mara defended.

"True or not," Matri said, coming to her, "it gave Nehushta her first chance to get back at Benoni."

Mara's heart sank. She withdrew and walked to the door. Beyond, the gate to the courtyard, usually hospitably open, was closed and barred. Above the wall and eastward, she could see the faint smudge of torchlight as the Roman soldiers moved back and forth dispersing the crowd. She felt tired, empty; and once more wondered if the misfortune which trailed her everywhere was about to influence Benoni's future, too. Misfortune had persistence. It picked its targets without seeming rhyme or reason. Had it already picked Benoni, too, as a target?

She turned back into the room. "I cannot stay here. It will bring shame and enmity into your house, Matri, as it already has brought it into the house of my master."

"But you cannot leave now," Shua said in alarm. "Matri's strength and influence as town elder would become suspect. We have given you our friendship. We would never turn you out. Not now."

"Not under such circumstances," Rakem added. "Besides, you have done nothing wrong."

"But the villagers all think I have," she insisted. "Don't you see how I am shaming you all?"

Matri walked to the table, sat down, and rubbed at his beard. "You must not be hasty, my child. We need to talk to Benoni before any decision is made or any action taken. Just be patient."

"And who knows," Rakem said, "Benoni may decide to take you to Perea with him."

"Perea? He's going to Perea? What for?" Mara asked in surprise.

"Is he planning that trip so soon?" Matri sounded as if he already knew all about it.

"Why is Benoni going to Perea?" Mara asked again.

"Some special business with the Romans about road taxes. The centurion who came to see him today was negotiating a price. That's when you came bursting in crying."

Anger flared. "I didn't know where else to run!" she snapped.

Rakem came to her. "Don't be angry. It's all right. You did right. Don't be afraid."

But as he spoke the words, someone rapped at the courtyard gate. Her heart began to pound. Instinctively, she moved to the farthest corner of the room and pressed hard against the wall.

Rakem exchanged quick glances with Shua and Matri, then went to stand protectively beside her.

Matri went out through the courtyard to the gate. Almost immediately he returned with Benoni, who carried a torch given him by one of the soldiers. Its light penetrated all areas of the room and clearly defined the fear-stricken Mara and the protective Rakem.

"Is the woman of brass still in charge of the streets?" Matri asked.

"Not now. The Romans are in charge. For the moment, anyway." Benoni handed the torch to Shua, mopped at his perspiring face, went to the table and sat down.

Matri and Rakem joined him. Mara remained unmoving. Shua laid the torch down over the firepit and disappeared into the inner room.

"The streets are empty and quiet. But only because the Romans are patrolling them. Once they leave, the protests and stonings may start again."

"How do we protect Mara?" asked Rakem.

Shua reappeared with a flagon of rum and three cups which she set on the table before the men. Matri poured, and they drank.

Rakem wiped at his mouth with the back of his hand, and asked again. "How do we protect her?"

Benoni glanced over his shoulder toward the unmoving Mara, and motioned for her to come to him.

She did so without hesitation, and knelt at his side.

"How quickly can you prepare for a journey?"

"Are you sending me away?"

"No. How quickly can you prepare?"

"Very quickly, master."

"Then do so. And keep the burden light. We will be traveling fast." Benoni turned to Matri. "My thanks to you for taking care of the tax collections here. Hire someone you trust to help you. The royal treasury will pay you."

"When will you return?" Shua asked.

"Not for many days." He turned again to Mara. "A Roman soldier waits at the gate to take you to my house so that you can pack for the journey. Rakem will go with you, too."

"As will I," said Shua, getting her shawl.

Mara retrieved the torch from the firepit, and led the way into the dark and hostile street.

Matri followed them and latched the gate. When he returned to the house, he said, "By taking Mara with you, people will think you are running away from trouble."

"And they'll be right, my friend!" Benoni paced back and forth. "Except for one thing."

"And what is that?"

"I want you to tell the men of the village that the Romans have ordered me to Perea. That is truth. You can also tell them that I have taken Mara with me, fearing it dangerous to leave her here. That, also, is truth!" He stopped pacing. "I want you to tell them one more thing."

"And that is?"

"Tell the men of the village that Nehushta is diseased."

Matri stared at him.

"Tell the men of the village that Nehushta has been with too many men, and that it is no longer safe to take pleasure with her."

"Is this also truth?"

"The warning should be given."

"But is it truth?"

Benoni shrugged. "Do you want Sychar to be rid of Nehushta, as I do?"

*Mara scrambled to her feet.
Rakem and Benoni stood still,
staring at the healed man.*

7

THE ANCIENT TERRITORY of Perea was located between the eastern shore of the River Jordan and the districts of Gerasa, Philadelphia, and Heshbon. On the north, the city of Pellas was its boundary. On the south, the fortress-palace of Machaerus established the border against which pressed the Nabatean kingdom. The River Jabbok cut through the territory east to west, draining into the River Jordan near the fording place which connected Perea to Samaria. The Perean road, in which Benoni had so much interest, followed the Jordan's eastern shoreline southward.

The sight of the River Jordan was an amazement for Mara's eyes. Benoni and Rakem had given her no warning of what to expect. And she had never seen such a powerful river. Nor, for that matter, any landscape quite like that which laced its banks. Strands of willows, acacias and tamarisks threaded the length of the river, creating a thick, green barrier against the rough hill country of Samaria on the west and the sandy desert lands of Perea on the east. Intermingled with the trees were wild cascades of flowers, water grasses, reeds, and thick rafts of papyrus. The sound of living water filled the air. She heard its rush even before they began to descend into the great valley through which the river flowed. The closer they came to the river, the warmer and more humid became the air until the whole valley seemed filled with the perfume of its life-giving moisture. She gasped in delight at the unfamiliar and unexpected.

"It is near this place, Benoni, where my friends tell me the Nazarene and his disciples are baptizing people," Rakem said, as they stopped at the river's edge. "Shall we look for him? He should not be hard to find. I am told that great crowds follow him."

"Later, perhaps," Benoni answered, looking up and down the river. "Where exactly is the fording place into Perea? That's where we're to meet my Roman friends on the eastern shore."

"The fording place is there." Rakem pointed upstream a short distance to a place where the willows seemed to grow out into the river.

They began to walk in that direction with Benoni in the lead. Mara caught up with Rakem. "What, or who, is a Nazarene?" she asked him.

Rakem laughed. "The Nazarene is a 'who.' The Nazarene is a man named Jesus. He comes from

Nazareth in Galilee. He is a teacher, a rabboni. Some people even think he might be the Jew's Messiah."

"The Messiah?" she repeated in a whisper. Samaritans, too, believed that such a savior would come someday. She even believed it herself. But she found a sense of surprise winding through her mind at the idea that Rakem might believe it. She had never thought of him as a religious man. She looked at him carefully; then at Benoni, and wondered what he believed. It seemed certain, remembering all the times he had talked about religion and politics, that he would consider the idea of a messiah as foolishness. She wished now she had asked him about it. Or maybe she should have asked Shua and Matri what they knew of Benoni's beliefs. Not that it would have changed anything. She was really quite content to be Benoni's woman, in spite of what his personal belief about God might be, in spite of Nehushta, in spite of the villagers, in spite of everything.

They neared the fording place. She could see that the land flattened into a natural clearing. The trees which earlier had appeared to grow out into the watercourse of the Jordan actually were on the river's eastern bank, and marked the place where the River Jabbok joined the Jordan. The water was shallow and clear. Wading across would not be hard. Benoni stopped and searched the eastern shore for his Roman friends. They were nowhere to be seen. He put down the pack of scrolls and writing tools which he had carried on his shoulders all the way from Sychar. For a man of his importance, he could have made Mara carry them. But he hadn't. She must find a way to thank him for that.

Rakem put down the small pack he carried, and she carefully set down her own bundle which consisted of almost the same items with which she had started her journey to Sychar—a small cheese, a round loaf of brown bread, a small waterskin, and her treasured doll. The shawl, which Cousin Nehushta had so roughly taken back from her, had been replaced with a new one from Benoni.

She had barely settled herself comfortably on the ground when she realized that there were other travelers on the trail. A group of seven or eight people approached the fording place from the eastern bank, and began to cautiously make their way through the shallow waters.

As the first man completed the crossing and stepped onto the Samaritan side of the river, Benoni hailed him. "Greetings and good day."

The man waved. "It is a day the Lord has blessed."

"How so?"

"We have seen a miracle performed this day."

"A miracle?"

By this time, a second man had completed the river crossing and came near. The first man pointed to him. "This man was healed of leprosy this morning. That is a miracle, is it not?"

A gasp escaped from Mara. She scrambled up onto her feet and stepped back. Rakem and Benoni, however, stood still, frozen in astonishment, staring at the healed man.

The man threw back the hood of his robe so that all of his face might be seen. He held out his hands that they, too, might be seen. There was not a blemish, nor a mark on either his face or his hands. The skin was smooth, youthful looking. His eyes held a look of radiance and joy. "It is true. I received a miracle this day. And I praise the Holy God for it."

"This miracle . . . who performed it?" Benoni asked, incredulous.

"Did the Nazarene called Jesus heal you?" It was Rakem who said the name even before the healed man could answer.

Benoni glanced at him in fresh astonishment.

Mara stared as if seeing Rakem for the first time. How could he know about such things? He'd just told her that Jesus was a teacher, not a healer!

"Am I right?" Rakem asked, walking up close to the healed man.

"You are right, sir. It was Jesus who healed me."

"And he healed many others, too, of diverse diseases," the first man said with open enthusiasm. "But only our friend here stayed to thank Jesus, and to witness to his great power. The others ran away, delirious with happiness and shouting 'Look at me, I am healed.'"

"It was Jesus who healed me," the leper repeated.

"Where did this happen?" Rakem asked.

"Not far from here, on the shores of the Jabbok." He turned and pointed back in the direction from which he'd come. "Jesus' disciples are baptizing people. But it was Jesus, himself, who healed me of my leprosy. It is a miracle."

"But what did he do? How did he do it?" Benoni wanted to know, as the rest of the group came up to join the first two.

The man shook his head. "How can one know how a miracle is done?"

"But what did he say to you? Did he touch you? What did he do?" Benoni insisted.

"I asked him to heal me. I told him I knew he had the power to do it, if he would."

"And—"

"And he said to me, 'Your faith has made you whole.'"

Benoni waited, expecting more of an explanation. But the man said nothing more. He simply looked at Benoni as if what he'd already said was the explanation and should be understood as such. "That's all he said to you— 'Your faith has made you whole'?"

The man nodded.

"And that's when it happened? That's when you were healed?"

"That's when it happened!"

"How did you feel?"

"I felt as if a great burden had been lifted from me. I felt free. I looked at my hands. They were smooth and clear of the festering sores. My friends here told me my face was clear."

"Were you his friends while he had the leprosy? Or are you just now his friends, since he is healed?" Rakem's question sounded sarcastic.

Benoni frowned.

But the healed man smiled. "They were all my friends before. While I had the leprosy. We are all from the same village up near Scythopolis. I asked them to take me to find Jesus. I knew in my heart he had the power to heal me. And he did."

"Where did you say Jesus was?" Rakem asked.

"Not far in that direction," the first man said, pointing back across the river. "A league or two. Not too far."

As they looked in the direction he indicated, three Romans rode into view.

"Ah, my Roman friends have arrived." Benoni made a respectful salaam to the healed man and his friends.

Rakem did likewise. "Your healing is wonderful. What a blessed day!"

Feeling weak with excitement, Mara picked up her burden of belongings. She scarcely could believe all she had seen and heard. The wonder of it all almost completely filled her mind. Yet, there remained one part of her mind that struggled with the reality of it. True, she had seen the man's unblemished hands and face. True, too, she could not doubt the sincerity of the look of radiance and joy in his eyes. Why, she wondered, could she not fully believe that this miracle had happened?

Rakem motioned for her to come and pick up Benoni's pack. "Do not let Benoni be shamed in the eyes of the Romans for carrying his own pack."

She did so at once, and hurried as fast as she dared to pick her way across the rock-strewn fording place.

The three Romans were on horseback. It added height to their uniformed figures, forced a person on foot to look up to them, and to give obeisance to them as if they were gods. With his short stature, Benoni seemed their victim.

The sight of them towering over him repelled Mara. A shudder went through her. She knew few of the details of his business with the Romans, but she feared for his safety. She knew in her bones that he should be wary in his dealings with these men of power.

"Greetings to you, Commander Lucius Marcellus."

"And to you, Scribe of Sychar."

He spoke with a slight lisp, which Mara found ominous. But much more ominous was the short quirt which he stuck into the top of one boot as he dismounted and handed the reins to one of his companions.

"Have you found a place for collecting taxes on this road?"

"I have, sir." Benoni walked away a few paces and pointed to a nearby spot. "This is a natural resting place for travelers. It should be a natural for collecting taxes from them."

The commander slowly followed after him. The afternoon sun glinted uncertainly on his helmet.

"Have you another location in mind, Commander?" Benoni asked, curious about the Roman's hesitancy.

"A thousand pardons, scribe. My mind is distracted. A league or two north and east of here is a well-sheltered crossing of the Jabbok. There's a gathering of people at that place who say they are followers of John the Baptizer. Do you know anything about them?"

Benoni gave the commander a narrow look of caution. His answer was indirect. "I heard that the Baptizer was in prison."

"So he is." The Roman pulled the quirt from the top of his boot and twirled it in an authoritative fashion. "Do you know anything about this gathering of his followers up on the Jabbok?"

Benoni shook his head. "Is that a location you prefer for the collection of taxes, Commander?"

The Roman turned on him. "Don't be a fool, man."

Benoni stiffened. His face became expressionless.

Mara and Rakem looked at each other, surprised at the Roman's abrupt hostility and a little frightened by it.

"What do you know about that band of beggars gathered up on the Jabbok, baptizing other beggars, and in general, disturbing the peace?"

"I know nothing about them."

"Those men you were talking to when we rode up . . . did they come from that gathering? Were they telling you about it?"

"They were asking directions, Commander," Benoni lied without hesitation.

The Roman looked at Rakem and Mara. "You there!"

Rakem straightened. "Me, sir?"

"Yes, you. What do you know about the gathering back there on the Jabbok?"

Rakem looked puzzled, and shrugged.

"And what about you, woman? What do you know of this gathering?" He pointed the quirt at her.

Fear paralyzed her, left her speechless.

The Roman gave an impatient curse.

Benoni confronted him. "We know nothing about a gathering on the Jabbok."

"Who are these people?" he demanded, pointing to Rakem and Mara.

"My deputy and my houseservant." Benoni walked toward him. "Why do you question me, Commander? We are supposed to be partners in the collecting of taxes on the Perean Road."

"We have to be very careful," the Roman rejoined. "A crowd like that on the Jabbok can easily turn things to a civil riot."

Benoni laughed. "In the wilderness of Perea?"

Color rose in the commander's face. "You set up the tax collection shelter wherever you like, scribe. I'll expect my share of the collections as we have previously agreed." He turned, went to his horse, and shouted for the other two soldiers to mount up.

"Where are they going?" Mara whispered to Rakem.

"To break up the gathering where Jesus and his disciples are teaching and healing."

"Will there be violence?"

Rakem nodded.

She cringed inwardly. "Shouldn't we try to warn Jesus and his men?"

Benoni overheard the question. "No! We came here to set up a tax-collecting booth. We did not come all this way to get involved with some religious fanatic."

Mara put down the packs and sank down next to them. Her heart was heavy and confused. She had experienced much that was new — a man who claimed healing from leprosy, a Roman commander obviously alarmed over a gathering of believers, and Benoni's single-mindedness about the collection of road taxes. She needed time to consider all these new things and try to understand them. Even more, she needed to try to understand how they would affect her life. She knew in her heart they would.

*If Jesus could bring peace to her,
she wanted to meet him. But how?*

8

FOR THE NEXT FEW DAYS they remained on the east bank of the Jordan, setting up the tax-collecting booth and collecting taxes from all passing travelers. Rakem taught Mara how to harvest papyrus from the rich growth along the river. It was a busy time. But even with new chores, Mara had much to think about during these days.

Sooner or later, Commander Lucius Marcellus would want an accounting of the taxes. He would most likely claim that Benoni was cheating him, and would challenge Benoni's records. Benoni would resent the challenge and, in some way, force the issue.

But concerned as she was for what might happen between Benoni and the Roman, other thoughts weighed on her even more heavily. They were thoughts which had to do with the healing of the leper, and the man called Jesus of Nazareth.

The mere idea that a leper could be healed by faith was startling and not understood, thrilling but questionable, exciting but unbelievable. Who was the man who had been healed? By what special choice or privilege did he claim healing and receive it? Was he an especially righteous man? Did he follow the great commandments without failure? Did he never lie or cheat or steal or lust after another human being? Was he a man good fortune merely smiled upon?

And what of this man called Jesus of Nazareth? Who gave him the power to heal? What kind of man was he to say the words, "By your faith you are healed"? Was he a magician using words of magic? Was he the only person who could do such things? She remembered once hearing of a magician in Sebaste named Magus who had enormous powers. Were there others, too, besides this Nazarene?

Or was it all some powerful blasphemy? Was it arrogance for any man to even claim such power? No god she'd ever heard of would so bless a mere man. She thought of her own plight, and all her seemingly unanswered prayers to her own One True God.

Yet, who was she to say that such things as healing by faith were impossible? Who was she, indeed, to even deny such a possibility in her thoughts? After all, she was only a woman; a woman who was continually followed by bad omens and worse misfortune. She remembered her brother-in-law's condemnation: "You wear misfortune like a shroud, Mara." And she shuddered remembering it, even now in this place of greenness and fresh hope far from Tabeal and far from the rejection and abuse she'd experienced in Sychar.

But aside from all such memories, why should she doubt that healing by faith was possible? She had seen the healed man. What further proof did she need? If she had no faith, at least she had proof of the claim. She had seen the leper with her own eyes. She had observed his clean, clear, youthful skin and the look of radiant joy in his eyes. If such a look was an outward expression of an inward feeling, as she had always believed, then what she had seen in the healed man's eyes was what she wanted for herself. If Jesus could bring that sense of peace to her, she wanted to meet him. But how? He was a Jew. And Jews avoided Samaritans.

She did not discuss her feelings or ask questions of either Benoni or Rakem. She knew how each of them felt. Rakem believed. Benoni did not.

She had overheard them talking. "How do you know the man really was a leper?" Benoni had asked Rakem. "How do you know that the Nazarene didn't pay the man to claim healing?"

"Pay—? The Nazarene? What for?" an angry Rakem demanded.

"To tell all the people that for a price the Nazarene could heal them, too."

Rakem snorted. "The Nazarene does not get paid for what he does!"

Benoni scoffed. "You talk like a woman, Rakem, as innocent and childlike as Mara. Everybody gets paid for what they do! One way or another."

"I tell you the Nazarene asks for no pay."

"Very well, have it your way," Benoni said, walking off. "But the very idea of it is beyond logic!"

When they returned to Sychar, Mara hurriedly sought out Shua and Matri to tell them what they had seen and heard, and to ask her questions of them.

They listened to her, intense interest in their eyes. As she finished her account, she asked, "Have you ever heard anything so — so — "

"Amazing?" Shua supplied the word she searched for.

"That's it. Amazing. Have you ever heard of such an amazing thing before this?"

Shua shook her head.

Matri, on the other hand, stood up and paced the length of the room, a thoughtful look on his face. When at last he spoke, his tone of voice was as distant as the memories he was recalling. "When I was a very young lad, a prophet came through our village. He spoke of a future time when someone would come who would be possessed of all kinds of power. This man would have the power of knowing our thoughts before we spoke them, the power of healing, even the power of resurrecting the dead."

Mara's eyes widened at the very idea. To be dead was to be dead. How could the dead be made to come alive again?

"The prophet spoke, too," Matri went on, "about a new kind of kingdom that was to come, and of a messiah who would lead men to it. He urged my father, who was the elder of the village in his time, as I am in mine, to tell all the other men of the village to study the sacred scroll, and to reshape their lives in accordance with God's great commandments."

Shua clasped her hands together as Mara had seen her do when she prayed. "Do you think that the Nazarene is the one spoken of by that prophet, my husband?"

Matri rubbed at his beard. "It is possible."

"It is very like the same message we have heard from John the Baptizer, isn't it?" Shua said.

Matri smiled at her. "Was there mention of the Baptizer, Mara, by anyone you met on your trip?"

"Only when the Roman commander told Benoni that John was still in prison at Machaerus."

Silence settled in the room, leaving each of them with their own thoughts. Mara reminded herself that it made little difference whether she actually believed in Jesus' powers. She would most likely never meet him. And even if she did, she doubted that his powers could help her. How could his powers be strong enough to dispose of the shroud of misfortune which was hers from birth?

The sound of the gate opening broke the silence. Shua got up, went to the door, and returned with Benoni and Rakem. They greeted Matri.

"You found your house in order, Benoni?" Matri asked.

"I did. And my gratitude to you and Shua for looking after things."

Matri pulled a money pouch from his tunic, smiled at the weight of it, and handed it to Benoni. "The taxes I collected in your absence."

Benoni thanked him, opened the pouch, poured out a handful of coins, and gave them to Matri. "This will reimburse you for all your trouble."

"You are a generous friend. And your house, Rakem? All is well there, too?"

"All is well, Matri. My thanks to you and Shua for watching after it."

Shua brought in a flagon of rum. Mara brought wooden cups from their storage place, and then joined Shua near the firepit.

"What other news do you have for us, Matri?" Benoni asked.

"The Roman soldiers patrolled the village for two days after you left. Then they returned to their road building west of Mt. Gerizim. They are still encamped near there."

"And so the hue and cry over Mara has quieted?"

"It was not fully quieted until two days past when Nehushta finally left Sychar."

"Nehushta? Left Sychar?" The questions popped out before Mara realized it. "Where has she gone?"

The men glanced at her in surprise.

Shua motioned for her to be quiet.

She ignored both reactions. "Where has she gone?"

"I don't know," Matri said. "I know only that she is no longer in Sychar."

A knowing look passed between Matri and Benoni.

"Why did she leave?"

"The men of the village demanded it," Matri said in a flat tone.

Mara glanced at Shua for a better explanation. But Shua was studying the embers in the firepit, and seemed disinclined to return the questioning look.

"Why did the men demand that Nehushta leave?"

Matri's face darkened with color. "It is not a thing to discuss with a woman." He glanced at Benoni and Rakem, then got up and walked to the doorway where he stood looking out into the waning light of late afternoon. "Light the lamps, Shua. Darkness approaches."

Shua lighted a small torch in the embers from the firepit, and went around the room lighting several tallow oil lamps.

"Why did the men of Sychar demand that Nehushta leave?" Mara repeated, feeling as if she was once more a stranger in this house.

"Nehushta had a sickness," Benoni said in a low tone without looking at her. "I asked Matri to tell the men about it."

"And they made her leave the village," Matri added from the doorway without turning around.

"What kind of sickness?" By the time the words had left her lips, she knew what kind of sickness they were talking about, and she regretted having asked. What she also regretted was that Matri did not know where Nehushta went. Though none of the others in the room realized it, her own life might well depend on whether or not Nehushta had gone to Sebaste, the city from which Mara had fled.

Benoni was looking at her with a strange expression, almost as if he recognized the fear she was feeling.

She wanted to tell him all about her past, all about her fears. She wanted him to know, and to reassure her that all would be well, that she need not fear. But how could she tell him? She had not even told him that she was married to Coniah, let alone that she was mortally afraid of him. If Nehushta should happen to go to Sebaste, she would learn about Coniah. Such knowledge in the hands of this vengeful woman could be very dangerous.

*This Roman's eyes harbored
no look of cruelty or craftiness . . .*

9

"HO, THERE! Woman. You. At the well!"

Startled, Mara turned, and shielded her eyes against the glare of the noontime sunlight.

A Roman soldier rode toward her on a sorrel horse.

Where had he come from? she wondered. And why was he traveling during the heat of the day? Romans hated Samaria's heat, and normally would avoid traveling in it. Just as she would, normally, avoid drawing water from the well at this time of day. Her reason for being here at this unusual time was because of the trouble she had had with the women of the village.

Except for Shua, of course. But she no longer went to the well with Shua, feeling it unfair to the older woman.

So far as the other village women were concerned, she was an outcast. They would not speak to her. They would not let their eyes meet hers. They bunched together, blocking her from getting close to the well. Finally, Benoni threatened their husbands with another raise in taxes unless they made their wives stop harassing Mara. From then on, she could get to the well. But as soon as she would draw one bucket of water, set it on the ground and try to fill the second, the first would have been kicked over and spilled.

It simply was easier to come to the well at a time when none of the other women were there. Since she was afraid of the dark, she chose to come when the sun invaded the uppermost part of the heavens and flung its heat across the earth like a mantle of winter wool. No one else came at this time. Except for today. Today, a Roman on a sorrel horse was coming toward her. Why was he here at such a time?

"Which is the road to Sychar?" the Roman asked, removing his helmet and mopping the sweat from his face and head. His hair was as thick and dark as her own. But his skin was much lighter. And his eyes were lighter. They were gray, light gray.

She put down the yoke with the leather water buckets attached, and carefully looked at the Roman. He was not really handsome. But he was important looking. And he was somehow different than many other Romans she had seen.

To be sure, his face had the hard, determined look of a soldier about it. It was square of jaw. The nose was aquiline. The cheekbones were high. But this Roman's eyes harbored no look of cruelty or craftiness, as had the eyes of Commander Lucius Marcellus.

His helmet was adorned with an eagle insignia unlike any she had seen before. His breastplate gleamed in the sunlight as if made of wrought silver. The short tunic showing beneath it was made of the finest linen. Even his sandals were different from the heavy clog boots worn by other Romans.

"Which is the road to Sychar?" he asked again, motioning to the fork in the road a short distance from them. "Do you know which it is?"

This time he spoke in Aramaic rather than Greek. He was indeed a different kind of Roman, she thought in surprise, and pointed to the road leading to the left, toward Sychar's houses shimmering white against the foot of Mt. Gerizim.

"And the Roman encampment? Where is it?" he asked.

She pointed toward the east-to-west road that cut through the valley between Mt. Gerizim and Mt. Ebal. "It is just beyond the shoulder of the mountain."

"Are you from Sychar?"

She hesitated.

He smiled, as if understanding her reluctance.

She found the reaction disturbing, and remembered Benoni's warning about not trusting Romans. "No matter how clear the look in the eyes, a Roman is not to be trusted," he had told her. "No more than Jews are to be trusted. Samaritans should always remember that. Even Samaritan women. Especially Samaritan women!"

"Are you a tax collector?" she boldly asked.

He laughed. "Do I have the look of a tax collector?"

"You might."

The Roman put his helmet back on and got down off the horse. "I seek a man in Sychar named Benoni-bar-Micah. Do you know such a man?"

She nodded cautiously, wondering why he wanted to see Benoni, hoping there was no trouble.

He pulled a waterskin from the pommel of his saddle and walked toward her. Without being asked, she took his waterskin and filled it from one of her own leather buckets.

"Thank you for your kindness." He drank. Behind him, the horse snuffled and pawed at the ground with one hoof. The Roman removed his helmet again, poured a quantity of water into it, and let the horse drink.

The action touched Mara. She considered it an act of kindness rather than necessity. She felt more confident of this Roman. "I know the man named Benoni. He is a very important man in Sychar." She refilled the leather bucket.

"And so he should be, since he is Herod's official scribe. Do you know where I can find this important man?"

"Oh, yes," she said proudly, throwing all caution to the winds. "I know where you can find him. I am his woman. I will take you to him." She attached the leather buckets to the yoke, slipped the yoke about her shoulders and went toward the village.

The Roman walked along beside her, leading his horse.

Benoni's reaction to the appearance of Tribune Bernardus was apparently similar to her own, she decided. She rather liked the idea that her assessment of the Roman's importance was confirmed by Benoni's immediate cordiality.

In contrast to the cool formality he had shown Commander Lucius Marcellus, he seemed jovial and hospitable with Tribune Bernardus. He invited him into the main room of the house, offered seating near his writing desk, and ordered Mara to bring cups of rum and a basket of bread and cheese.

"Did you come all the way from Caesarea-by-the-Sea especially to see me?"

Mara placed the basket of food, cups and a flagon of wine on Benoni's writing table between them.

The Roman took off his helmet and put it down on the floor. "I came from Jerusalem to see you."

"I didn't know that a man of tribune rank was stationed in Jerusalem."

"It's a new post. I am the liaison for Pontius Pilate to the court of Herod Antipas." He sipped at his rum.

Benoni sipped at his own cup to cover any sign of astonishment he felt. It was most unusual for a man of such high rank to call on a toparchy scribe. In fact, it was so unusual that caution overpowered any sense of flattery which he might at first have felt. "That's an impressive post. In the name of all the gods, how can I be of help to you, Tribune?"

"Actually, you can be of help to me in two ways." The Roman put his cup on the corner of Benoni's writing desk, and leaned forward, elbows on knees, in a confidential manner. "In the first instance, do you know about the beheading of the Jewish prophet?"

"Jewish prophet? You mean the man called John the Baptizer?"

"The same."

"I didn't know. When did it happen? And where?"

"It happened five days ago. At Machaerus."

Benoni put down his own cup, and wiped his hand across his mouth. The news was unwelcome. In the eye of his mind, images of the dauntless prisoner he'd seen at Machaerus remained strong and real. To hear that the man was dead was oddly saddening. To learn the man had been beheaded stirred anger deep inside him. "At whose order was the beheading done?"

"It was ordered by Herod Antipas during a drunken orgy. But – " The tribune hesitated, narrowing his eyes in an unseeing stare, his thoughts clearly far-distant.

Benoni motioned for Mara to come and refill the Roman's cup. Then he gently urged, "But what, Tribune? Was someone else responsible, too?"

"Yes. Someone else was responsible."

"Herodias?" Benoni's voice was almost a whisper. "And you were there, weren't you, Tribune?"

"I was there. I saw it all. Herodias goaded Antipas. And finally, she tricked him into having the act done. And when it was done, Herodias ordered the executioner to present the head on a platter of silver to Antipas."

Fresh anger cut through Benoni. There was nothing he could do about what had happened to the Baptizer. But he felt revulsion toward Herodias, and a scornful pity toward Antipas. For the Roman sitting across the desk from him, he felt a curious sympathy. "You said I could help you in this matter, Tribune. What did you mean by that? How can I help you?"

The Roman's eyes slowly lost their far-distant stare. He straightened and sipped at the freshly filled cup. "You can help me, or I should say you can help Governor Pontius Pilate, avoid another killing."

From the corner of the room, Mara stifled a gasp of astonishment.

Benoni threw a warning glance at her, and then shifted around on his chair to get a better look at the Roman and to make certain he had heard him right. "Help Pontius Pilate? Avoid another killing? How can I do that?"

"Do you know anything about a Jewish uprising?"

"No. I don't."

"Pilate is receiving reports that such an uprising is being planned as a show of outrage and protest against the beheading of the Baptizer."

"I've heard nothing here."

"Not even among the travelers and caravan people who come along these roads?"

Benoni shook his head, thinking how similar these questions were to those asked at the gathering of the scribes many weeks before.

"What about in Perea?"

Again, Benoni shook his head. "Why do you ask about Perea?"

"Because it is your toparchy. And because I understand you were recently in Perea."

Benoni could remember a time when he would have been flattered by having a high-ranking officer know about his activities. But in this instance he found it disturbing.

"Commander Lucius Marcellus has sent in a report that you might know something about such an uprising."

"Why should I know about such a thing?"

"Why were you in Perea?"

"To set up a tax collecting booth on the Perean road."

"Nothing more?"

"Nothing more. But why should you ask?"

"Commander Lucius Marcellus expressed concern that you had not reported the gathering on the Jabbok where a friend of the Baptizer's was preaching."

Benoni stared at the tribune in complete bafflement.

"Commander Marcellus also wrote that all of Herod's toparchy scribes were ordered weeks ago to report any such gatherings. Were you not at the meeting at Machaerus?"

"I was."

"Then why did you not report this gathering at the River Jabbok?"

"Because Commander Marcellus knew of it before I did. In fact, he is the one who told me there was such a gathering. He and his men passed by it on their way to meet me on the banks of the Jordan."

New understanding crept onto the tribune's face. He took a piece of cheese, broke off a piece of the coarse brown bread, wrapped it around the cheese, and began to chew on it.

Benoni glanced over his shoulder toward Mara. Her fascination at hearing all this conversation clearly showed in the rapt expression on her face. Benoni warned her with a look to remain quiet.

The tribune finished chewing, and reached for another piece of cheese.

"Did Commander Marcellus not report to you that I met with him for that purpose?"

"He did. But I should like to hear your report of it."

"The commander seemed much more interested in the gathering at Jabbok. In fact, he was alarmed by it. Helping us build the tax collection booth seemed secondary. He said he feared a civil riot."

"And that was all?"

"That was all."

"Didn't Commander Marcellus tell you he needed your help in breaking up the gathering? That there was such a crowd that it resembled a street mob?"

"A street mob?" Benoni laughed aloud. "How could any gathering on the banks of the Jabbok resemble a street mob?"

A peculiar expression came onto the tribune's face, making it obvious that he had never been to that particular part of Perea.

"It is open country," Benoni explained. "Within a very narrow distance of the river, the growth of trees and grasses stops. There is nothing beyond but a desert-like landscape. Even with thousands of people gathered together, it could not resemble a street mob."

An embarrassed flush appeared on the Roman's face, now making it obvious that Commander Lucius Marcellus had given a report quite different.

Benoni turned, motioned for Mara to bring more cheese and bread and another flagon of rum. "May I commend you, Tribune?"

"For what?"

"For being so thorough as to check out rumors. Especially since your post is a new one. And since it is a very important post. Yes. I respect you for your diligence."

The tribune gave a wan smile. "I am discovering this new post is much more complicated than I expected."

Benoni, feeling more relaxed, now helped himself to the cheese and bread. "You mentioned there were two ways I might be of help to you. What was the second way?"

The Roman ran one hand through his hair and softly laughed. "Oddly enough, scribe, the second problem I have also has to do with Commander Lucius Marcellus."

"Oh?"

"The problem has to do with the man's identity. I have yet to meet him face-to-face. I plan to go to Tiberias from here to do so. But in the meantime, since you have met with him and know what he looks like, is this the man you call Lucius Marcellus?" From a leather pouch attached to his belt, the Roman pulled forth a small cameo and handed it to Benoni.

It took only a moment's study of the finely carved stone before Benoni handed the cameo back to the tribune. "The man whose face appears here is unknown to me."

"And yet you have met face-to-face with this man from Tiberias called by the name Lucius Marcellus?"

"I have. But the face on the cameo is not the man I know by that name."

The Roman nodded as if expecting such an answer, and when he spoke again there was a certain sadness in his voice. "The face on the cameo is a likeness of the real Lucius Marcellus, however."

Benoni arched an eyebrow. "The real Lucius Marcellus?"

Tribune Bernardus nodded. "The real Lucius Marcellus is my brother."

Benoni looked thunderstruck.

Mara's gasp of astonishment went unnoticed.

"How long have you known the man who claims to be my brother, scribe?"

"Not long. A few weeks," he hesitated, and corrected himself. "Several weeks, I suppose. He came one day before khamsin, and that has been several weeks ago. In fact, more like several months ago, now that I think back."

"He came to you here? From where?"

"From Caesarea-by-the-Sea as I recall."

"Why did he seek you out?"

"He said he was on his way to Tiberias as the new commander of that garrison. He said his orders had been damaged in an accident, and he needed them recopied on a new parchment."

"Did he show you the actual damaged orders?"

"What was left of them. The parchment had been badly torn, as I remember."

"Then how did you know what to copy on a new parchment?"

"He told me what to write."

"Ah-h-h . . . that was convenient, wasn't it?"

Benoni began to feel uncomfortable. If the tribune felt he had forged the man's orders . . .

"Whose signature of authorization did he tell you to use? Do you recall?"

"The signature of Pontius Pilate, I believe. But that I could see on the damaged parchment. That he did not have to tell me."

"And you're sure that the name he claimed as his own was Lucius Marcellus?"

"Quite sure."

Tribune Bernardus sat quietly for a long moment, staring across the room, deep in thought.

Mara looked at Benoni, wanted to go to him for reassurance and to reassure. But she knew it would not be the thing to do.

Tribune Bernardus stirred. "Will you go with me to Tiberias and point out this imposter to me?"

"Well . . . I . . . uh . . . "

"I can order you to do so, Benoni-bar-Micah."

It sounded like a threat. Mara held her breath.

"I hope I will not have to do that, however."

"Of course, Tribune, of course. It's just that the tax collections here are . . .   But no matter, I'll get my friend Rakem to take care of that business. When will you want to leave?"

"At first light tomorrow." He picked up his helmet and stood up.

Benoni led the way out of the house and across the courtyard.

A new shudder of alarm went through Mara. New trouble was yet to come. She knew it in her bones. The Roman she had thought to be so different from the others might turn out to be the most troublesome of all.

On a reflex so swift and involuntary that it surprised even her, Mara slapped the old woman full in the face.

10

LONG AFTER TRIBUNE BERNARDUS took his leave of Benoni's house to stay overnight at the Roman encampment on the far side of Mt. Gerizim, Mara continued to think about all she had heard. From time to time during the afternoon, she looked at Benoni working at his desk, and wondered at his ability to maintain an outward calm that in no way betrayed the fear and confusion he must surely feel. She admired him for that. For herself, she felt like hiding in a corner and crying. Her old companions of misfortune and trouble were now pursuing Benoni.

Even throughout the next day, long after Benoni and the tribune had left on horseback for their journey to Tiberias, she continued to worry about him. Her prediction of trouble with the Roman commander that she had felt when she saw him in Perea had become a reality. What could she do to help Benoni? What, indeed?

She wished she knew more of the details of his business dealings. But she could only guess at them from overheard bits of conversation with Rakem. The only thing she knew for sure was that the commander held his post in Tiberias because of documents Benoni had forged for the man. That was bad enough.

But now, to learn that he was an impostor compounded the possibilities for trouble should it all be discovered. And it would be discovered. The tribune was determined. And Benoni was at his side, within arm's reach, when the truth would be revealed in Tiberias.

She thought again of how much she admired Benoni's ability to hide his feelings. And in a way, she was amazed at it. As amazed as she was at the boldness of the man who called himself Lucius Marcellus. Bold had to be the word that described him. For he went about everywhere as Lucius Marcellus. According to Benoni and Rakem, he'd even gone to the scribes' meeting at Machaerus under that name. Did no one in Judea or Samaria or Galilee know the real Lucius Marcellus?

How could such a bold person be successfully confronted or trapped? She began to tremble again as fear for what might happen to Benoni overruled her sense of reasoning. And in her fear, the most obvious facts escaped her. Benoni was guilty of only one thing. Forgery. Who the impostor really was didn't affect Benoni. Whatever had happened to the real Lucius Marcellus didn't affect him, either. But in her fear, such reasoning did not occur to her. All she could think was that her own misfortune was once again affecting Benoni. "Misfortune, misfortune, be gone from me," she murmured.

In spite of her pleas, misfortune continued to cling to her. It seemed to her as if it was a living thing, determined to increase its presence in her life and dominate her.

On the second day after Benoni's departure from Sychar with Tribune Bernardus, Hodesh appeared at the gate of the house asking to see Benoni. "I need him to read a letter for me." She waved a small parchment in the air.

"He is away," Mara said, not opening the gate wide enough for Hodesh to enter.

Curiosity flashed in the old woman's eyes. In a loud voice she asked, "Away? Why is Benoni away? Away where?"

When other villagers who were passing by turned to look, uneasiness crept over Mara. "He will return soon," she said, trying to sound reassuring as well as loud.

"I will wait!" Hodesh pushed against the gate.

"Then wait in the street," Mara resisted, trying to close and latch the gate.

"You have no hospitality."

"You deserve none."

Hodesh pushed harder with unexpected strength, forcing Mara to give ground.

Rakem came hurrying from the house, aroused by the sounds of the argument. "You are not welcome here," he said, blocking Hodesh.

She glared at him with disapproval.

"What is it you want?"

"She wants someone to read a letter for her," Mara said quickly. "You can read it for her, can't you, Rakem?"

"I can."

Refusing the offer, Hodesh shoved the parchment into the folds of her cloak.

"Rakem reads as well as Benoni," Mara challenged.

Abruptly, Hodesh straightened. A suspicious look replaced the determination on her face as she studied Rakem for a moment. Then suddenly she asked: "Does Benoni know you're here with his woman?"

The implication of the question caught them both by surprise.

The suspicious look on Hodesh's face slipped into one of accusation. She gave a thin, sneering laugh, and wagged her finger at Mara. "Isn't one man enough for you?"

On a reflex so swift and so involuntary that it surprised even her, Mara slapped the old woman full in the face.

It caught Hodesh off-balance. Screeching, she grabbed for the gate to keep from falling.

Rakem rushed forward to help her. She shoved him away and lunged at Mara, missing her as Mara dodged. Hodesh sprawled on the ground at her feet.

"I have had enough of your ugliness, Hodesh. You have caused me great hurt. Your gossip and rumors have made me an outcast. No woman in the village, save for Shua, will be my friend."

Hodesh struggled to free her feet from the tangle her own cloak. Rakem made no further move to help her. She swore, got up onto her feet, and made her uncertain way toward the gate. "You will regret this, Mara. You will regret it."

Mara ignored her and went into the house.

Rakem dispersed the crowd that had gathered in the street with a wave of his hand, and closed the gate behind Hodesh. By the time he returned to the house, Mara had her shawl and her doll in her hands and was making a food bundle. "What are you doing?"

"I am leaving this place. I can do nothing but bring misfortune to everyone who befriends me."

Rakem went to her, and with firm gentleness made her put down the doll and the shawl and the food bundle. "You have not brought me misfortune. Nor have you brought misfortune to Benoni. You defended my honor and his, as well as your own."

She shook her head. Tears filled her eyes.

"Believe me," he said, taking her by both arms and looking squarely at her. "You cannot leave Sychar now. It would give the victory to Hodesh."

From behind her, she heard footsteps coming through the rear entrance to the house and through the inner room. In the next instant Shua appeared, a worried frown creasing her face, making it obvious that the news had already reached her.

"Talk to her, Shua," Rakem pleaded. "Make her see how foolish it would be to run now that she has stood up for herself against Hodesh."

"Is it true that you slapped Hodesh?"

"I did." Her tone was almost defiant.

Shua began to smile, slowly at first, and then more quickly until at last, she threw her head back and gave a great laugh.

Mara felt confused. She had never seen her friend act like this. And certainly, she had expected no such reaction considering the circumstances. She glanced at Rakem. He, too, was now grinning and seemed on the verge of laughter. Her confusion increased, and she began to think they were laughing at her, making fun of her. With a sinking feeling in her heart, her eyes filled with fresh tears and she started to turn away.

Shua stopped her. "Every woman in Sychar has longed to put Hodesh in her place. But you are the first to have the courage to actually do it."

Mara stared in astonishment.

"Believe me, my child." Shua pulled a linen square from her tunic and brushed at Mara's tears.

"Now do you understand why you cannot leave Sychar?" Rakem asked, coming closer. "Now do you see what foolishness that would be?"

"We are your friends, Mara."

"But you're laughing at me."

"We laugh because we think Hodesh got what she deserved," Rakem corrected.

"The other women may not make friends with you, Mara, but most of them will stop treating you as an outcast," Shua said, handing the linen square to her.

Mara wiped the last of the tears from her eyes. "You really think so?"

"I really think so."

"And so do I," Rakem said. "And when Benoni returns from his journey with the tribune, he will no longer worry about your safety when you fetch water from the great well."

The reassurances from Shua and Rakem lifted her spirits. But their predictions of an end to harassment by the women of the village proved to be wrong.

On the very next morning after the incident with Hodesh, Mara found a dead rat carefully laid on the threshold of the doorway leading into Benoni's house. For it to have been put there meant that someone had to climb the compound wall.

Two days later, as she made her way to the stream to bathe, someone followed her and stole the homespun cloak which Benoni had given her when she first came to his house. Later the same day at noontide, on her way back from the great well, Nehushta accosted her.

"Where did you come from?" Mara exclaimed, as Nehushta stepped from behind a small tree to block the path to the village.

"It's where I've been that is important."

Mara waited, tense, on guard.

"Don't you want to know where I've been?"

Not knowing whether to stay or to run, Mara waited. The leather buckets suspended from the wooden yoke across her shoulders were heavy with water. It made running almost impossible.

"You surprise me, Mara. I thought you would at least be curious about where I have been all these weeks since Benoni's lie about my health turned the men of Sychar against me."

Mara suddenly found her voice. "What lies? You are an unclean woman. That is no lie."

Nehushta's eyes glinted with anger.

"And anyway, why should I care about where you've been?"

"You and Benoni should care. You are both affected by where I have been."

"Leave Benoni out of this."

"But you are his woman!"

Anger boiled up inside Mara. "Say plainly what you want, Nehushta. And then be gone!"

Nehushta straightened in surprise.

"Say what it is you want."

"I want you to ask me where I have been."

"I don't care where you've been." She turned to go on into the village.

Nehushta blocked the way. "I have been to Sebaste."

Mara froze.

"And there I met a man named Coniah."

Coniah! The name crashed into Mara's mind.

"Does Benoni know that you have a husband?"

Helpless, she stared. Benoni had said he wanted a woman he could trust. She thought she had become that woman for him. Now, she realized she had not, could not, become that kind of woman for him. Oh, if only she had been honest with him in the first place!

"No need to answer my question. I can see by your face that you have told Benoni nothing about Coniah!"

With Nehushta's laughter chasing her, she turned and fled into the village.

The Holy City adorned the heights of Mount Moriah and Mount Zion.

11

JUST INSIDE THE CITY GATE, Mara stumbled and fell. The water from the leather buckets spilled, soaking her tunic and sandals and making a small mire of mud in the dusty street.

Matri, and two citizens sitting with him in the gate talking, saw her fall. They got up quickly and came to her. "Are you hurt, my child?"

"You should never run with a yoke like that on your shoulders," said one of the men.

"Nor should you run in the heat of the noontide," said the other man.

She shrugged free of the yoke and scrambled to her feet. "Nehushta is back," she gasped, pointing toward the gate.

The men turned in surprise.

"She will not dare to come into the village," Matri scowled.

"We'll chase her out if she does," said one of the men.

"Where is Shua?" Mara asked in panic.

"In the house."

She turned and fled, fear pounding at her as it had when she ran from Coniah.

"Mara! Wait! The yoke and buckets . . . "

She pretended not to hear. She must find Shua, and safety. But Shua was not in her house. Though she called and searched for her, Shua was not to be found. Fresh panic seized her. In desperation, she ran for Benoni's house. It, too, was empty. Then she remembered. Benoni was in Tiberias. Rakem was at the crossroads collecting tax from passing caravans. And Shua was nowhere to be found.

She was no longer safe in Sychar. She raced into the inner room and grabbed her treasured doll, ready to flee, to hide, to find safety somewhere else.

But where could she go? There was less safety outside the gate. Nehushta was outside the gate. And Coniah—where was Coniah? She stopped short, trying to control her panic, to put down the frenzy she felt.In an exhaustion of desperation, she sank to the floor, cuddling her doll.

It was there Shua and Matri found her and took her back to the safety of their own house. Toward the time of twilight, Rakem returned from the crossroads, and they told him what had happened.

"I wish we could take you away from Sychar again," he said. "Like Benoni did when he took you with us to Perea."

"I wish you could, too. But where could we go that Nehushta wouldn't follow?" she asked.

"You will be much safer right here in Sychar," Matri said. "Nehushta will not dare to come inside the gates again. She would not dare."

"But I am not really safe here. Not with Benoni gone," she protested.

"Of course you're safe here," Matri said in a firm tone, frowning at her with disapproval. "Where else do you have friends?"

"Friends or no, dear Matri," she insisted, "I am not really safe here. If I were, how could someone put a dead rat on the threshold of Benoni's house? How could someone have followed me to the stream and stolen my cloak? And why didn't someone warn us that Nehushta was waiting just outside the gate for me today? No, Matri, I do not feel safe here any longer."

"But where could you go and be any safer?"

"Where I am not known at all. Where I can get lost in a crowd."

"We could go to Jerusalem," Shua said softly.

Mara glanced at her in surprise.

"Jerusalem? In Judea? Away from Samaria?" Matri asked, an astonished tone in his voice.

"It is the only place I know of where a person can get lost in a crowd without fear."

"Benoni would never forgive us for sending her off by herself," Matri said.

"Why should she have to go alone, my husband?"

"Who would go with her?"

Shua simply looked at him, a gentle smile playing around her lips.

"You? You would go with her?" A perplexed look crossed his face. "What would I do without you?"

Shua rose to her feet and went to him. "You are the town elder, my husband. You can have the help of most everyone in this village. Our friends will help you until I return."

He frowned and shook his head.

"I don't mean to take sides, Matri, but one thing Benoni asked me to do while he was gone was to take the collections from the past weeks up to the scribes' treasurer in Jerusalem."

"Why do you think of this now?"

Rakem shrugged. "Traveling with two women at my side will make my journey safer. Who would ever guess that I carry money to Herod with only two women in my company?"

Matri looked doubtful. "It is too much of a risk."

"Money carriers always take armed guards with them. I will have only Shua and Mara. There is no risk."

Matri studied Rakem for a long moment.

"Whether or not the women go with me, I still must make the trip. I promised Benoni I would do it if he was gone more than three days."

"Who will see to the tax collections while you're gone?"

"Joab. I spoke with him this very day. He knows what must be done. You will not have to trouble yourself, Matri."

"How long would you have to be gone?"

"A week, perhaps. Certainly no longer. And by that time, surely, Benoni will have returned from Tiberias."

Silence settled over them, leaving each person to his or her own thoughts. Beyond the open door, a cloud shadow moved over the courtyard bringing with it a softening of late-lingering light. A gentle brush of air swirled along the hard-packed earth, circulating a tiny dust-dancer from the bake oven toward Dendo's hay crib before disappearing into a larger circle of air. In fascination, Mara watched it, thought how quickly it changed patterns, realized that her own life patterns were changing, and wondered if her destiny was to be as uncertain and as quickly disappearing as the small circle of dust.

Two days later, a different kind of thought went through her mind as she stood with Shua and Rakem on a hill looking at Jerusalem. The Holy City adorned the heights of Mount Moriah and Mount Zion like a diadem. Mara beheld its glory with a growing sense of awe. The great temple of white marble, adorned with golden parapets, sparkled in the sunlight of late afternoon.

No wonder the Jews claimed that the worship of the One True God should take place here, she thought. No wonder they scorned the Samaritans' place of worship on Mount Gerizim. There, the primitive stone altar looked small and alien in comparison with the magnificence before her.

"It is as if all of man's talents and honor were built into this place, is it not?" Shua asked the question in a tone of such reverence that it parallelled Mara's own sense of awe.

"You feel it too?" Mara asked.

"More now than the first time I beheld it."

"But, you're a Samaritan," Rakem said with a soft laugh. "And the wife of an elder!"

"That is true," Shua agreed. "But even I see something important in the Jews' great Temple."

Mara looked at her and saw that the expression in her eyes confirmed the respect and reverence in her voice.

"What is it you see?" Rakem asked.

"The Jews' great temple is an important and ancient symbol. It is a symbol of a person's need for a spirit greater than his own."

Though she could not have expressed it in words, Mara shared Shua's feeling. It was odd, she thought, looking again at the temple. It was designed to stir the highest feelings of worship. Even in the hearts of Samaritan women. Even in the heart of a Samaritan woman like herself. It almost made her forget what an unlucky woman she was, with doom and misfortune dogging her every footstep.

"Come along, you two," Rakem urged. "I want to find lodging for us before darkness drapes the land."

They went forward once more, following Rakem, and frequently side-stepping other travelers and their herds going in the same direction. Once inside the walls of the city, they made their way along the Street of the Damascus Gate. They passed the great Roman fortress that secured the northwest corner of the Temple Mount, and went down into the vale of the Lower City. Mara suddenly hesitated, hung back, almost overwhelmed at the number of houses, the crowds of people, and the noise of the market place when they passed through its narrow confines, brushing body to body and shoulder to shoulder against strangers.

"Come along, child," Shua urged, trying not to lose sight of Rakem who was pushing steadily through the crowds in front of them.

In a rush of panic, Mara grabbed for Shua's hand and let herself be led through the tightly packed passageways.

At last, Rakem paused in front of a doorway on which was a small wooden sign marked with Hebrew symbols. He rapped at the door, and in a very short time, it was opened by a young boy who gestured for them to enter. As they stepped through the doorway, the innkeeper, a burly man, came to meet them. He eyed the three of them first with curiosity, and then looked again at Mara with open interest.

"I seek lodging for the two women and myself," Rakem said.

"For tonight only?" the innkeeper asked.

"And perhaps for one more night as well," Rakem said.

"You are in Jerusalem on business?"

"I am." Rakem said this in a tone that invited no more personal questions. "What is the charge for your rooms?"

"Will the three of you share a room?"

"We will. This is my mother and sister," Rakem lied. We will share a room."

The look of interest faded from the innkeeper's face. "Will you require food, also?"

"We will."

"In that case, the charge will be three leptons each person for each night. And for more than one meal add three more leptons. I require the price of one night's lodging in advance."

Rakem found his money pouch, extracted nine leptons from it, and handed them to the innkeeper. "And where is this room?"

The innkeeper bit on one of the coins to test its worthiness, then pointed upward. "There. The shelter on the roof. The ladder is at the end of the courtyard." He cast another look of interest at Mara before turning and disappearing into the house.

"We'll be safer on the roof than anywhere else in his house, I would suspect," Shua said.

Rakem grinned at them both. "I'm glad you appreciate what a nice place I have led you to."

They found the ladder, climbed up onto the roof, and went to the shelter of palm-thatch in the far corner.

Several reed sleeping mats were stacked under it. They selected three mats, shook them and laid them aside along with their own belongings.

"Will you go yet this day to the scribes' treasurer, Rakem?" Shua asked.

He shook his head. "I think not. Darkness is close at hand. I will seek out the treasurer at first light. For now, I think it is best if I stay here with you and Mara. It has been quite a walk. We all need rest and something to eat. I'll go below and have the innkeeper's boy bring us something." Rakem disappeared down the ladder.

Mara walked to the edge of the roof and looked at their surroundings. The inn was situated halfway down the Cheesemakers' Valley in the Lower City. Many buildings of importance were visible around them.

Shua joined her, pointing them out. "Over there to the west is the great royal palace with its three towers. And there, a hippodrome, which the Romans find so entertaining. And there is the Fortress Antonia, and just to the east of it, the great Temple."

Mara turned suddenly toward her companion. "Shua, tomorrow could we go up onto the Temple Mount? To the Women's Court?"

Shua looked at her in surprise.

"When I was a little girl, I heard stories about it. I have always wanted to see it."

The look of surprise softened.

"Could we go and see the Women's Court of the great Temple for ourselves?"

Shua smiled.

Mara felt excitement growing inside her. "Could we make a sacrifice so that the One True God would take the awful burden of misfortune away from me?"

Shua's smile faded to a look of sympathetic understanding, and she reached out to her. "Of course, we will go. Of course, we will make a sacrifice."

"I have no money, but if Rakem would give me some until we return to Sychar, Benoni will repay him."

Shua patted her hand. "I have a few coins of my own. We will buy a sacrificial dove."

Mara shivered with excitement at the mere idea of it and at the prospect of finally being relieved of the awful specter of misfortune.

The next day when Rakem finished delivering the tax moneys to the scribes' treasurer, he took them to the Temple Mount. They entered by the great wide staircase on the south side of the structure, passing the pools designated for ritual cleansing by devout Jews, on through the Huldah Gates, and at last, to the stalls of moneychangers. Rakem purchased three small sacrificial doves in a reed cage. An inner stairway led from the stalls up onto the stone pavement where the Temple itself was located.

As they stepped out onto the spaciousness of the Court of the Gentiles, Mara gasped in astonishment at the spectacle, and stopped to stare. At this close distance, the Temple shimmered even more brilliantly than when she had first viewed it from the hills outside the city. Now, its pure white stones and golden adornments glared with so much reflected sunlight that she had to shield her eyes against it. She looked away to let her eyes adjust themselves.

When the effects of the brilliance gradually left her, she could see that all around them in the shaded area of the great colonnade called Solomon's Porch were hundreds of other people. Many, like themselves, carried cages of doves. Others had unblemished sacrificial sheep in tow. Some people were seated, silent in meditation. And still others, a great throng, seemed to be clustered around a rabbi, listening with great interest as he spoke of a new kingdom which was at hand.

Rakem touched her arm. "Come, Mara and Shua, the Women's Court is in this direction."

"Take care not to speak aloud," Shua warned. "Samaritans are not welcome there. It is truly only safe for us here in the Court of the Gentiles. Even the Romans and Greeks come here."

Enthralled and obedient, she moved along behind Rakem and Shua.

At the entrance to the gate of the Women's Court, Rakem paused, spoke to one of the priests, handed him the cage of three doves and a handful of coins. The priest nodded and went toward the altar where smoke from the burnt offerings was thick in the air. It smudged the view of the pure white Temple beyond. Rakem motioned for her and Shua to go on into the Women's Court. He turned away and went into the gate of the Men's Court.

Mara moved along behind Shua woodenly, almost overwhelmed by the idea of being in this place so honored, so esteemed, so revered, and so exclusive to the Jews. The Women's Court itself was a large paved open area surrounded on three sides by roofed galleries. It was the enclosure farthest away from the altar and the shining white and gold building that housed the Jews' treasures of worship. It was separated from the places of central religious action by the Men's Court and the Court of the Priests. For Mara, it didn't matter. She was here to sacrifice and pray. And she was closer to God's great Temple than ever before.

Many other women were already inside the enclosure. Some prayed aloud in the peculiar rhythm of the Hebrew dialect. Some gently swayed back and forth as if the physical action added important emphasis to their prayers. Still others stood quietly, arms upraised, eyes closed, murmuring as if to keep the privacy of their prayers to themselves. All the women wore face veils.

Shua pulled her own head shawl forward to mask her face, and motioned for Mara to do the same. Then she knelt to pray, hands clasped before her.

Mara knelt, too, affecting a posture like Shua's, but wondering how she could force her mind into any prayerful thought when she was so filled with curiosity; so eager to watch all the other women; so nervous at being in this important place of worship.

But she would try. The greatest wish of her heart was to be free of doom and misfortune. She closed her eyes, not knowing what to expect or what to say in her deepest heart that would sway the One True God. She coaxed her mind to concentrate on being free of doom and misfortune.

When that happened, Nehushta could no longer harm her. Coniah would not find her. All would be well. Surely, it was not too much to hope for, nor to pray for.

A pang of affection tugged at him.
Had he fallen in love with this waif
who had come to him out of the night?

12

FOR ALL OF THE MONTHS they had been together, Benoni had never had cause to question Mara's loyalty. She had, in every sense, shown herself to be a woman he could trust. He thought often of that; was pleasured by it, and quietly reveled in the feeling of assurance it gave him.

He was thinking of it now as he rode alongside Tribune Bernardus on the way back to Sychar from Tiberias, and he was reminded of how bleak his life had been before Mara. She was a strange mixture of innocence and insolence that satisfied him in all ways.

He no longer even wondered about where she had come from. Once, when he first brought her into his house, he had questioned her about her past. But a look of such deep fear had come into her eyes that he had not pressed her for an answer, and never again did he question her about her background. He had finally decided it did not really matter. He found her pleasing. She was the only family he had. And on this trip with the Roman, he had missed her.

He supposed he felt so keenly about family at the moment because of what had been learned about Tribune Bernardus's missing brother. He was missing for good reason. He was dead.

The real Commander Lucius Marcellus, brother to Tribune Bernardus, was dead, the victim of a freakish accident some months before involving a legionnaire and a muleteer in Caesarea-by-the-Sea. The muleteer had fled. But the legionnaire had buried the commander's body, and had taken on his identity. Later, he had paid Benoni to forge new documents for him and assumed the role of commander of the garrison Tiberias.

When confronted by Tribune Bernardus, the impostor quickly admitted the deception. He was stripped of his bogus rank and authority and imprisoned for impersonating a Roman officer. There was reasonable doubt about who actually caused the accident which had killed the tribune's brother. Much of that doubt focused on the missing muleteer. Bernardus, therefore, intervened on behalf of the legionnaire and spared him from being crucified.

Benoni glanced at the tribune riding in silence beside him. He was a man deserving of respect. Not many men would have given the benefit of the doubt to the legionnaire. But the tribune had. Yes, he was a man deserving of much respect.

And at the moment, he was a man deserving of sympathy, too. Lines of fatigue beyond the physical creased his face. His eyes looked sunken and dark with the misery of mortal loss. There was about him the desolation of rejection that comes to every man of feeling and sensitivity at the death of a brother. Such a desolate sense of rejection bridged differences in race and upbringing and stations in life. It was a mutually shared experience, a mutually understood feeling.

It surprised Benoni that he should feel such compassion for a Roman. Or that he should transfer such a feeling into a sense of family where Mara was concerned. But he recognized that somehow that was happening. His feelings were real. Especially his longings for Mara. He needed her because she needed him.

She needed his protection. He could only hope that she had not been pestered or frightened by the villagers while he had been away. And he further hoped that Rakem and Shua and Matri had given her whatever protection she might have needed.

He began to wonder if he should marry Mara. Perhaps that would help things. Certainly it would change her status. In the eyes of the villagers, she would become a moral woman if he made her his wife.

But marry? The idea of it disturbed him. Marry? He almost said the word out loud. Should he? Why should he? Marry? Would that solve Mara's problem? How would it affect his own status? And what new problems might it create for him? Marry? It was a foreign thought, one outside his self-perception, one beyond his need.

Tribune Bernardus reached the top of the last ridge of hills separating them from the valley where Sychar was located, and stopped. Benoni reined up next to him and looked down at the valley. Mounts Gerizim and Ebal stood as majestic landmarks on either side of it. The north-south east-west roads cross-hatched the short grass of the valley, filled it with travelers and livestock thirsting for the flowing freshness of Jacob's Well.

Tribune Bernardus shifted in his saddle. "You are almost home, friend Benoni. Your woman will be glad to see you."

Benoni grinned in spite of himself.

"I will leave you when we reach the well."

"But my house welcomes you," Benoni protested. "At least stay the night before going on to Jerusalem."

Bernardus shook his head. "I thank you for all your help. And for your kindness. It has been a sad and tiring trip. I am anxious to reach Jerusalem and publish warrants for the arrest of the muleteer."

"As you wish."

"One more thing I wish to say to you. Your identification of the impostor helped me discover what really happened to my brother. You should be rewarded in some way."

Benoni shrugged off the suggestion.

But the tribune insisted. "You must be rewarded. That is why I want you to keep the horse you have ridden on this trip."

Benoni straightened in surprise.

"Herod's scribe needs and deserves an animal to ride. He shouldn't have to walk everywhere in pursuit of his duties. If Herod won't supply you with a horse, Pontius Pilate, through his Tribune Bernardus, will do so!"

Benoni could not believe it. The gift was unexpected and much valued.

"This is the first time I've seen you at a loss for words, Benoni!"

Benoni bowed deeply, so deeply that his head touched the pommel of the saddle.

Bernardus chuckled. "Your actions speak louder than any words. I accept your thanks!" He urged his horse forward down the ridge into the valley toward Jacob's Well.

Benoni followed. When the horses were watered and the two men started to part from each other, Benoni said, "Once again, let me tell you of my sorrow for your brother and for your loss of him."

Bernardus nodded, quickly turned away to hide the tears that sprang into his eyes, and rode away.

Benoni watched him go; then, leading his fine new horse, turned toward the village and Mara. Because of Bernardus' generosity, they both now already had a new status among the villagers. The fine new horse would make it so.

Usually, regardless of how much time he had spent away from her, reunion with Mara was as if nothing had changed; as if time itself suspended movement, and they simply picked up their relationship at the same instant of understanding as before.

But this time things had changed. Mara's trip to Jerusalem, and particularly her visit to the Women's Court of the Temple, gave her new things to talk about, new bits of life to share with him, new ideas to try to describe before they lay together in intimacy.

She was as willing and responsive to his advances as always, but her newly expressed interest in prayer bothered him. What bothered him even more was to learn that Nehushta was lurking about again, and had caused Rakem to take Mara and Shua with him when he delivered the tax moneys to the scribes' treasurer in Jerusalem.

He got up from the reed mat, looked back at the still-sleeping Mara. A pang of affection tugged at him. Did he finally have even more special feelings for her than he had imagined? Were his feelings for her deeper than any he had known with any other woman? Had he fallen in love with this waif who had come to him out of the night?

He walked quietly to the doorway and looked out into the courtyard. The night had deepened, leaving the canopy of heaven star-flecked and silent. He stepped into the courtyard. His fine new horse raised its head and made a soft snuffling noise. He went to it, stroked its muzzle, and thought again of Tribune Bernardus and his burden of loss. What would he, Benoni, do if he lost Mara?

The question came spontaneously, uncalled, hard, and frightening. Why should he have such a thought? How could he lose her? he asked himself. Why, by all the gods, should he think such a thing? He turned swiftly, went to the outer gate, threw it open as if half expecting to see some monstrous demon standing in the street. But the street was empty, silent. He cocked his head, listening through the silence in an effort to pinpoint the source of the premonition of disaster which now overtook him.

"What is it, Benoni?" Mara asked the question in a voice as soft as her footsteps had been when she came up close behind him.

He turned with a start.

"Apologies, my master. I have frightened you."

He let out a sigh of relief. "I thought I heard something. But it is nothing."

A look of fear crossed her face. "Nehushta?"

"No. I was mistaken. It is nothing." He shut the gate and latched it.

She said nothing more, but Benoni knew that the fear was still inside her, sensed that she was not satisfied with his response. And why should she be? He was not satisfied, either. But what could he tell her? That he had been thinking about marrying her, and that a black premonition had overwhelmed him? He turned back toward the house with Mara silently following.

At earliest light, he slipped away from her once again, this time leaving by the doorway from the inner room at the back of the house, and made his way to Rakem's house. He knocked at the door with a quick one-two rap which Rakem would recognize as his own. Within seconds, the door opened revealing Rakem rubbing at his eyes and looking very sleepy.

He carefully pushed Rakem back a bit, stepped into the house and closed the door behind him. "I know it's early, but I need your help."

Rakem yawned and stretched. "Again? What this time?"

"I want you to find Nehushta."

Rakem straightened, wide awake by sheer astonishment.

"I want you to find Nehushta and bring her to me at Matri's house."

"But where would I look for her?"

"If she confronted Mara just outside Sychar's gates, as you told me she did, then she must be living somewhere close by. Maybe even as close as Shechem."

"But that's scarcely two leagues away."

"Exactly! Find her, Rakem. Find her. Bring her to me at Matri's." He left the house before Rakem could make further protests, and hurried back to his own place.

The morning seemed to creep by. He searched for things to do, and fought off impatience. But by the time the sun had climbed to its highest and turned the land into a cauldron of heat, he still had no word from Rakem. The search for Nehushta was obviously more difficult than he had expected. His impatience grew.

Mara noticed, supposed it had something to do with the sadness he felt for Tribune Bernardus, and kept out of his way as much as possible. But at last she had to approach him. She walked into the courtyard where he sat shaping new writing quills, though she herself had done a fresh supply before going to

Jerusalem. "I'm going now to fetch our water, my master."

He nodded distractedly without looking at her.

It made her wonder if she was the real cause of his aloofness rather than sadness for the Roman. But she didn't question him. She picked up the yoke and the leather buckets, left the courtyard, and walked toward the city gate. No breeze displaced the sultry heat. No villagers displaced the emptiness of the streets. As she expected, and wanted, her trip to the well again would be a solitary one. Even Matri and the men who usually sat with him in the gate to talk of important things were absent. The heat had driven everyone inside their houses.

She approached the gate and went through it slowly, alert and careful, remembering the day Nehushta had accosted her outside the walls with threats about Coniah. But today, Nehushta wasn't there. No one was there, except for three strangers coming up the trail toward the village.

She stepped to one side of the trail for them to pass. They appeared to be Galileans. All wore the distinctive seamless robes for which the weavers of Galilee were so well known. But why would Galileans be going into Sychar? Considering the ancient feud between Samaritans and all other people, Galilean visitors were infrequent.

As the three men passed, she heard the tallest of the three say, "Finding food may be a problem. I see no people in the streets. This may not be a market day in Sychar."

"Then we'll ask somebody, even if they are Samaritans," said the red-headed man, who appeared to be the youngest of the three. "I'm famished."

"Cheese and bread will be a feast," said the third man who was an older version of the red-headed one. Mara thought they might even be brothers.

She made no effort to help them or to give them directions to the cheesemaker's house or to the house of the widow Hodesh, who would sell bread to anyone. Even to a Galilean. Why should she help them? She stepped back onto the trail and continued her slow walk toward the well. Arriving there, she slipped out of the yoke and began to unloose the leather buckets.

It was then that the man spoke to her. With a start, she straightened and glanced around. He sat leaning against the trunk of a small tree growing near the well, with his back to her. She wondered how he knew she was there. But in the next moment, she decided it was the sound of the leather buckets being loosed from their yoke which had drawn his attention.

There was something faintly familiar about him. Did she know him? Was he someone who had come to pay taxes to Benoni? She decided not. She did not know him. He was a stranger. His hair was brown, the color of almonds that had been roasted. It was only of medium length, barely touching the back of the neckline of his pure-white linen tunic. His shoulders, broad and muscular, filled out the tunic seam to seam in such obvious strength that she was reminded of the gladiators she'd seen as a child in Sebaste.

She wondered if he was a gladiator. Beside him on the ground was a robe which appeared to be similar to those worn by the three strangers who had passed her on the trail. In all probability, this man, too, was a Galilean, she decided. And most likely he was a Jew as well.

"Please, would you give me a drink?" he asked, repeating his original question.

She laughed, considering the question a foolish one. Everyone knew that Jews did not speak to women in public. She remembered Shua telling her about some Jews who were called the "bruised and bleeding Pharisees" because they chose to shut their eyes and walk into a wall rather than look at a woman on the street. Even more importantly, Jews did not speak to Samaritans. Nor did Samaritans speak to Jews. How could she take this man seriously? The question was a foolish one.

The man turned and looked at her.

He was not unhandsome. His beard was neatly trimmed. But the thing she found most surprising was that the look on his face was one of extraordinary kindness.

Once more, he asked for a drink of water.

"Aren't you a Jew?"

"I am."

"Then how can you, a Jew, ask for a drink from me?" she repeated. "How can you ask for a drink from a woman? A Samaritan woman!"

"I thirst," he said simply, getting to his feet.

He was taller than she had expected. His arms and hands were as strong looking as his shoulders, and he carried himself with the tough leanness of an athlete.

Yet, there was nothing menacing about him. In fact, he appeared to be weary, as if he had walked a very long distance. She realized there was a presence about him that was causing her to stare at him very impolitely.

"Will you give me drink?"

She forced herself to look away, to fumble with the slender cords attached to the leather buckets and use their tangled state as a reason not to answer him.

"If you knew what God can give," he said, "and if you knew who it is that said to you, 'Give me a drink,' you would have asked him, and he would have given you living water."

His immediate reference to God caught her even more off-guard, made her feel belittled, even scornful. He must think she was as foolish as she thought he was. "Sir, you have no bucket. This well is deep. Where can you get your living water?"

She fumbled again with the cords on the buckets.

"Let me help you." He came to her.

She found his offer confusing. It made her more curious than ever. She let go of the cords and studied his face. It was tanned, weathered, with features which were regular, without special markings of a particular race. He could be Samaritan as easily as Jew, she thought. Or Greek. Or Roman. But beyond physical appearance, she sensed, even more powerfully, some strange presence about him. What was it that made him seem so different from other men?

Not even Benoni had this kind of effect on her. Not even he had this kind of presence. And Benoni was the strongest man she knew.

She stepped back and surveyed the stranger even more carefully, from the top of his head to his sandaled feet. He was powerfully built, but there was a softness about him, a gentleness, a presence of compassion. Was that what made him so different? "Sir, are you a greater man than our ancestor, Jacob, who gave us this well, and drank here himself with his family and his cattle?"

The man smiled at her and lowered one of the buckets into the well for her.

It was woman's work to draw from a well. He did it so naturally that it took her a moment to be astonished. He, a Jew, was doing woman's work. Jew or Samaritan, it made little difference. It was woman's work this man was doing! Yet he showed no hesitation, no embarrassment. What kind of a man was this? He must be mad.

She heard the bucket hit the water far below; saw the muscles in his arms tighten against the weight as the bucket filled; saw him strain, just as she always had to do, to pull the heavy bucket up again. What kind of man was this, indeed?

He set the bucket on the ground, carefully, spilling not a drop.

An unexpected pang of guilt came over her. She reached into the folds of her tunic, pulled forth a small wooden drinking cup, filled it from the bucket and handed it to him.

He gave her a nod of thanks, and drank.

Hurriedly, she picked up the second bucket and dropped it into the well.

He returned her cup, and said, "Everyone who drinks this water will be thirsty again. But whoever drinks the water I give will never be thirsty again."

"How can that be?" she asked, pulling the second bucket up from the depths of the well and setting it beside the first. "What makes the water you give so different?"

He turned, picked up both buckets, and motioned for her to pick up the yoke and follow him.

Without protest, she obeyed him.

He led her into the shade of the small tree and put down the buckets.

She laid aside the yoke. "What makes the water you give so different?" she asked again.

"My gift will become a spring in the man or the woman who receives it, welling up into eternal life."

She wasn't sure she understood what the words "eternal life" meant. But to never again be thirsty, to never again have to come to this well in the heat of the day, alone and isolated, still scorned by other women in the village, was something she did understand. It was a burden she wanted to be free of. "Sir, give me this water, so that I may stop being thirsty, and not have to make this journey to draw water any more!"

"Go and call your husband, and then come back here," he said to her.

"I don't have a husband." She answered with such quick honesty that she surprised herself.

"You're quite right in saying you don't have a husband," he replied, sitting down again in the shade of the tree.

Mara remained standing, feeling that to do otherwise would be somehow disrespectful to him.

"You have had five husbands," he went on, "and the man you have now is not your husband at all. Yes, you spoke the truth when you said that."

She stared in astonishment, wondering how he knew these things about her. Someone must have told him. But who? Did he come from Sebaste? And what else did he know, she asked herself. Maybe he knew everything—how she attracted doom and misfortune and rejection, how terrible her marriage to Coniah had been, and her awful fear of telling anyone in Sychar about it, even lying to hide it. She even wondered if he knew that none of her prayers to be rid of her misfortunes had been answered. Not even the prayers she said at the great Temple in Jerusalem. And then the thought entered her mind that maybe he knew why her prayers had not been answered.

But she was afraid to ask directly. She would have to be cautious, find another way to get at it. "Sir, I can see that you are a prophet!" she began.

He neither confirmed nor denied it.

She went on with her circumspection. "Now our ancestors worshipped on the hillside there, but you Jews say that Jerusalem is the place where men ought to worship, and—"

He interrupted her. "Believe me, the time is coming when worshipping the Father will not be a matter of 'on this hillside' or 'in Jerusalem.' "

"Not have a special place to worship? Not have an altar? Not have rituals and make sacrifices?"

He gave her a steady look without replying.

She felt free to go on, in spite of the fact that talking with a strange Jewish man was outside any other experience of her life. "You Jews are more strict about rituals and making sacrifices than we Samaritans."

"Nowadays you are worshipping what you do not know. We Jews are worshipping what we know, for the salvation of mankind is to come from our race. The time is coming, yes, and already has come, when true worshippers will worship the Father in spirit and in reality."

As though urged by some inner voice, she asked without hesitation, "Are you illusion or reality?"

He smiled. "Indeed, the Father looks for men and women who will worship him in spirit and in reality. In spirit and truth. For God is spirit. And those who worship Him can only worship in spirit. That is truth. That is reality."

"You talk as Messiah might."

"You know about Messiah?"

"Of course. All Samaritans know about Messiah," she returned. "He is the one who is called Christ. When he comes, he will make everything plain to us."

He looked at her for a long moment, then spoke quietly, confidently. "I, who speak to you here and now, am Messiah. I am Christ."

And then he glanced away, gazing into some distant future not open to her. The expression on his face altered, became pensive and reflective of such an awful rejection that Mara's own heart trembled with sadness.

*"Very well. I will go with you.
But I refuse to believe that any man
is a god."*

13

MESSIAH? Could it really be?

She stood unmoving, unsure of what she heard, uncertain she understood. Prophet, yes. Man of wisdom, yes. A teacher, yes. But Messiah? Could it really be?

Then she remembered that the Baptizer had proclaimed the coming of Messiah. Rakem had told her about it. So had Shua and Matri. Even Benoni scoffingly had told her what many other people were saying.

"What is your name?" she asked in hushed breathlessness. "Where do you come from?"

"My name is Jesus-bar-Joseph. Nazareth is where I lived for many years. But now, my Father has called me to teach and preach and heal."

"Nazareth? Jesus of Nazareth? You are the Nazarene?" she exclaimed. "I've heard of you. My friends have heard of you, too. You're the one who healed a leper!"

The pensive look in Jesus' face went away. "There are many kinds of healing for those who believe."

She sat staring at him, unable to believe in her good fortune. "You are the Christ? And you have told me?"

"You are the first I have told," Jesus nodded.

"Why? Why me?"

"Why should I not tell you?"

"But I am a woman, and a Samaritan. You should hate and despise me."

"Why?"

"Because . . . because . . . it is custom. From the days of our fathers and their fathers before them, it is custom."

He smiled as he might at an over-serious child. "Go now. Get the man you're living with and come back here."

She turned, ready to do his bidding, and saw that the three men who had passed her earlier on the trail were standing at the edge of the tree shade. The red-headed one carried cheese and bread. The tallest of the three carried a flagon of rum. She suspected he had bought it from Matri. Looks of bewilderment filled their faces. She knew it was because Jesus was talking with her. She also knew, instinctively, that they would not question him about it. How could they? They were his followers. They believed in him. If they had watched him heal a leper, how could they question him about talking to a woman? A feeling of joy went through her. She straightened, swaggered a bit as she had seen Benoni do, and with a nod of deference to them all, hurried back up the trail and into the village, as eager to tell the good news to everyone as to fetch Benoni.

The first people she saw was the widow Hodesh and her son-in-law. She hailed them, excitedly told them about Messiah being at the well, and ran on to find Benoni, not caring that Hodesh laughed at her in derision, or that the son-in-law cursed in disbelief.

She burst through the outer gate of Benoni's house, calling his name, expecting him to still be in the courtyard working at shaping quills. But the courtyard was empty. Not even the fine new horse was there. The house was empty, too, and she wondered if Benoni had left the village for some reason.

She debated this for only a moment, though, and then hurried to the house of Shua and Matri. They would know where Benoni was. As she hurried along the street, she passed two of the men who sometimes sat in the city gate discoursing with Matri. Both of them looked harried and hot. One of them was mopping the perspiration from his face, for midday heat still smothered the land. She hailed them.

They looked at her in surprise, since she never before had spoken to them.

"Go to the well," she called out. "See the man who may be the Anointed One of God."

They looked at her as if they thought she was deranged.

She ran on, unconcerned at their reaction, more eager than ever to find Benoni, Shua and Matri, and Rakem, and tell them all about her remarkable encounter with the Nazarene.

Shua was in the courtyard, pulling fresh-baked bread from the oven. Opposite, the little donkey Dendo shared his patch of shade with Benoni's fine new horse.

"Shua! Something wonderful has happened! Where is Benoni?"

Startled, Shua juggled the hot bread, almost dropping it. Benoni appeared in the doorway of the house. Matri and Rakem were just behind him.

Mara ran to him, laughter in her voice. "Benoni! Come quickly to the well. He is there!"

"Who is there?"

"A man who has told me many things I have done!"

"What man?"

"Jesus. Jesus of Nazareth. The Nazarene!" The words tumbled from her lips in a spate of joy.

Benoni's eyes went wide in astonishment.

Rakem pushed past his friend and grabbed Mara by both arms. "The healer is here?"

She nodded.

Rakem let out a yell of delight and twirled Mara about in a dance.

Shua and Matri exchanged stunned looks, then began to smile. "So . . . the prophecy is coming to pass in our lifetimes," Matri said with such satisfaction that Benoni's look of astonishment turned to one of open curiosity.

"What does he mean?"

Mara pushed away from Rakem, went to Benoni. "That means that Jesus of Nazareth is Messiah."

Benoni scoffed. "And he spoke to you?"

"He says I am the first that he told!"

"Why you?"

"Because I am woman. Because I am Samaritan."

Benoni shook his head.

"Don't you see? If I believe, any and all will believe, too!"

Benoni remained unconvinced.

"He told me to bring you to meet him."

"I must go to meet him, too," Matri said. "As village elder, I must offer to him the hospitality of all Sychar."

"Go in my place, old friend," Benoni said, stepping away from Mara. "I believe in Roman gods, not in Jewish myths."

Mara's heart sank.

"Benoni!" Rakem admonished. "Close your heart, if you will. But keep your senses open!"

"Mara asks very little of you," Shua firmly reminded him. "It will not hurt Herod's scribe with the fine new horse to meet this man."

"It will not hurt you to offer the hospitality of your house, either," Matri said. "You would do that for the lowliest of travelers!"

"You are all against me!" Benoni declared in angry surprise.

"We are reminding you to be your best self, my friend," Rakem said stoutly.

Mara came to him and whispered, "I love you, Benoni. And Jesus has asked me to bring you to meet him. Please come."

He looked at her for a long moment, and as his anger cooled he recalled the awful fear that had come on him earlier when he thought of losing her. "Very well," he said gruffly. "I will go with you. But I refuse to believe that any man is a god."

By the time they went out from the city gate, many others were already heading toward the well. But as the word passed that Matri was coming along behind them, they paused and stood aside out of respect for his office as village elder, so that he and those with him might arrive first at the well.

When they reached the edge of the scant shade where Jesus and his companions were resting, Matri halted and salaamed.

Rakem leaned close to Benoni and Mara and whispered, "Those are the men who bought rum from me earlier today."

The Galileans all rose to their feet acknowledging Matri's greeting. There was an unusual presence about all of them, but it was Jesus to whom all eyes were drawn.

"You are the Nazarene?" Matri asked in his most formal manner.

"I am," Jesus replied.

"And I am Matri, village elder. I bid you welcome to Sychar, and I offer you the hospitality of our village."

"It is kind of you." Jesus turned to introduce his companions. "This is Simon, called Peter."

The tallest of the three nodded.

"This is John." Jesus pointed to the redhead. "And this is James, brother to John."

The two brothers bowed.

"We four are on our way back to Galilee to meet the rest of those who serve me as disciples. They await us in Capernaum where we have much teaching to do."

"We, in Sychar, would like to learn from you, too, great teacher," Matri said. "Will you sit with us and tell us of the fulfillment of the prophecies?"

"There are many things to share," Jesus agreed. Then, turning, he smiled at Mara. "These are your friends?"

"They are," she said, excited that he should direct conversation to her in front of everyone. "This is Shua, wife to Matri. This is Rakem. And this . . . " She turned, tugged at Benoni's sleeve, urging him forward. "This is Benoni. He is Herod's scribe in Sychar. And he is my master." For the merest instant, she wished she hadn't said Benoni was her master. After all, if Jesus was truly Messiah, he was master.

But contradicting her did not seem to be in Jesus' mind, for without hesitation he made a sweeping motion and asked, "And what of those? Are they your friends, too?"

She turned to see the rest of the villagers coming down the trail and across the fields toward them. Most of them had ostracized her, especially the women. None, she felt, were her friends. But when she turned again to face Jesus, she said, "They are my neighbors, sir."

The answer seemed to please him.

Benoni stepped forward with sudden boldness. "The hospitality of my house is yours while you are in Sychar, Nazarene, if you care to accept it."

Jesus looked at him carefully. "It will not trouble you?"

Benoni shrugged. "If it will not trouble you."

"To be troubled by such generosity is to think unclearly. My men and I welcome the hospitality of your house, Benoni."

"I have never seen you smile so much,"
Shua whispered to her on the second day
of Jesus' visit.

14

MARA COULD SCARCELY BELIEVE that for the next
two days, she and Benoni were hosts to the Nazarene
and his men. She was so filled with joy that life did not
seem real. Peter, John and James went separately about
the village talking with people and teaching, as Jesus
had taught them to do, while Jesus sat in the gate of the
village with Matri, discoursing with the men and teaching them. At night, Matri opened his courtyard and his
house so that the entire village might hear Jesus preach.

His preaching was much like his teachings to the
men during the daytime. He spoke about things of
everyday life; things that the people of the village could
understand because of their own experiences. He spoke

of many things. But some of them Mara took to her heart to remember and think on later.

On the first night, Jesus spoke in a parable about a lamp on a stand. "No one lights a lamp and hides it in a jar or puts it under a bed. Instead, he puts it on a stand, so that those who come in can see the light. For there is nothing hidden that will not be disclosed, and nothing concealed that will not be known or brought out into the open."

Reminded of what she was hiding in her own life, Mara shivered a bit and glanced toward Benoni sitting across the room with Matri and Rakem and other men of the village.

"Therefore," Jesus went on, "consider carefully how you listen. Whoever has, will be given more; whoever does not have, even what he thinks he has will be taken from him." Did this mean she would have to go back to Coniah? She shivered again, and looked at Jesus. She found his words unsettling. She had expected something more comforting from him. She was trying her best to make a better life for herself; to rid herself of the shroud of doom and misfortune. She had to believe that meeting Jesus would make that happen.

The very fact that Jesus and his men were guests in Benoni's house thrilled her. It seemed even more important than Jesus' preaching. And she reminded herself that the changes brought about by the presence of such important houseguests were almost unbelievable. Her own chores of cooking, baking and drawing water from the well increased. But she was astonished at the help she was offered. Shua, of course, was the first. Then two of Shua's oldest friends. Then came others who had never before spoken to her. And each brought a gift of food for Jesus and his men — bowls of lentils, loaves of freshly baked bread, baskets of corn ripe on the ear, cheeses, olives, melons and grapes.

Mara now went to the well in the early morning when the other women did. None of them ignored her. Many of them even spoke to her. Some said to her, "At first we were only curious because of your talk about Jesus. But now we ourselves have listened to him. We know he really is the savior of the world." Overnight, she had become a woman of importance. She was no longer ostracized and scorned.

"I have never seen you smile so much," Shua whispered to her as they served the evening meal on the second day of Jesus' visit.

"He makes my heart sing," she replied. "And just look at how differently Benoni is acting!"

"There is a difference in Matri, too," Shua said, glancing over her shoulder to the table where the men were all seated. "And there is a difference in Rakem. It is as if new life has been given to them."

"Of course, Rakem was a believer before Jesus came," Mara reminded her.

"Now he will believe even more strongly, and be blessed."

"I know Benoni doesn't believe in Messiah, but he likes and respects Jesus. I wonder if he will be blessed, too."

On the second night, when the evening meal was over, they all went to Matri's house to hear Jesus preach in Sychar for the last time. He spoke first about being ready to enter the kingdom of heaven. He likened it to a story about ten virgins.

"At that time the kingdom of heaven will be like ten virgins," Jesus said, "who took their lamps and went out to meet the bridegroom. Five of them were foolish and five were wise. The foolish ones took their lamps but did not take any oil with them."

A titter of laughter drifted among the women at his description of a familiar experience.

Jesus smiled at them, nodded, and went on. "The wise, however, took oil in jars along with their lamps. The bridegroom was a long time in coming, and they all became drowsy and fell asleep.

"At midnight the cry rang out: 'Here's the bridegroom. Come out to meet him!'

"Then the virgins woke up and trimmed their lamps. The foolish ones said to the wise, 'Give us some of your oil, our lamps are going out.'

"'No,' they replied, 'there may not be enough for both us and you. Instead, go to those who sell oil and buy some for yourselves.'

"But while they were on their way to buy the oil, the bridegroom arrived. The virgins who were ready went in with him to the wedding banquet. And the door was shut.

"Later, the others also came. 'Sir! Sir!' they said. 'Open the door for us!'

"But he replied, 'I tell you the truth, I don't know you.'" Jesus paused as the effect of his story settled on the crowd. "Therefore, I say to you, keep watch, because you do not know the day or the hour."

As Jesus finished the story, there was no further laughter among the women. The truth of it was too real. The application of its wisdom for the kingdom to come was too frightening.

Jesus straightened and smiled at all those who were gathered at Matri's house. "I thank you all for your hospitality these past two days."

Matri rose to his feet. "The thanks must go to you, Rabboni, for the truths you taught us, for the days of fulfillment yet to come. But there is one final question I must ask."

"And what is that?"

"Of the commandments in the Law, which is the greatest?"

Jesus replied: "Love the Lord your God with all your heart and with all your soul and with all your mind. This is the first and greatest commandment. And the second is like it: Love your neighbor as yourself. All the Law and the Prophets hang on these two commandments."

A hush had settled over the gathering as Jesus spoke. It continued for several moments after he finished speaking. All the people sat looking at him, drawn to him in respect, even Benoni, and absorbed by the odd presence which emanated from him.

At last, he stood up, repeated his thanks to all for their hospitality, and with his three men, left Matri's house.

Benoni and Mara caught up with them in the courtyard and escorted them to Benoni's house.

As Peter, John and James began to climb the ladder to the roof where they had slept each night, Jesus turned to Benoni and Mara. "Come up and sit with us a while. The air will be cooler on the roof. Come up and refresh yourselves. We will talk."

"You are not too tired?" Benoni asked, for the press of the crowd at Matri's had been greater than ever. The news of Jesus' presence had spread and people had travelled from other villages to hear him.

"Only my body is tired," Jesus answered. "But the cooler air will refresh me, as it will refresh us all. Come."

When they reached the rooftop, John gave a great sigh and lay down full length on the hard-packed flatness of the roof. Peter lolled near the ladder. Next to him, James sat with his arms encircling his knees and his head resting on them. Jesus sat down and leaned back against the short wall engirding the flat roof like a parapet.

Benoni and Mara seated themselves nearby as good friends would do. Starlight's soft silver sheen overspread the roof. No one spoke. Below them, the streets of the village were now silent, too, except for the occasional bark of a keen-eared dog. Refreshment was as much in the silence as in the cooler air of the rooftop.

Mara leaned back against the short wall, thinking what a miracle had been wrought that allowed her to even be here on the roof with them. By custom and tradition, she should never have been included. But with Jesus, custom and tradition, in some ways, seemed to no longer matter. So far as he was concerned, she was as welcome as Benoni was to sit with him and his men.

It was a miracle, indeed. If this, too, was a part of the new kingdom which Jesus had preached about, then she supported the whole idea. But she wondered what would happen when his new kingdom came into power. Would Herod Antipas and the Romans fight it? What would happen to Benoni's job? Would he still be as important as he was now?

She looked over at Jesus. Even at rest, she could feel the strange power that surrounded him, that drew people to him in spite of themselves. But would this power, this presence, be enough to make his new kingdom a reality, she wondered? How would he do it? He had no soldiers like Herod Antipas. He had no legionnaires like the Romans. If he was just a carpenter from Galilee, then he had no money, either. How could he and the three men who were with him possibly bring this new kingdom into power?

Apparently, Benoni's thoughts were similar to her own, for it was he who broke the silence with a question. "What of your other disciples, Jesus? Those who await you in Capernaum? What are their names, and how long have they been with you?"

Jesus roused. "The others are nine in number. They have been with me almost from the very beginning of my public ministry here. Their names are Thomas, Nathanael, James the Small, Simon the Zealot, Andrew who is a natural brother to Peter, Judas of Keriot, Matthew, Bartholomew, and Philip. The three you see before you, however, were chosen first. The others were chosen very soon afterward."

"They are all Jews?"

"They are."

James raised his head, and looked at Benoni. "Does that bother you?"

"I'm not sure. If you are Messiah, Jesus, as you told Mara you were, then to whom else are you Messiah? To the Romans? To Greeks? To Persians? To Damascenes? Or just to Samaritans and Jews?"

Mara's heart curled up inside her. How could Benoni be so rude? How could Jesus help but be offended by such words? She looked at him, fearful to see anger in his face. But there was no look of anger, only a look of calculated measurement of Benoni's sincerity.

"I wondered about that myself, Benoni," Peter spoke up. "But I have had a chance to see that Jesus is Messiah to anyone who believes him to be that. That is his identity. There are those who choose not to believe. But that doesn't change it."

"He is also a friend to every man, and . . . " John said, tilting his head in Mara's direction, "and to every woman, as well, it seems."

"If he were not friend to all," James said, "we would not be sitting here on the roof of your house!"

"Nor would we have spent two days as your guests," John added with a laugh. "You Samaritans!"

"I am not Samaritan," Benoni cut in quickly. "I am Greek. A Greek from Delos."

"And whose gods do you believe in?" James wanted to know.

Benoni did not answer.

"I, too, would like to know that, Benoni," Jesus said without rancor. "What or whom do you believe in?"

Benoni continued his silence for a moment longer, then said in a thoughtful tone, "I suppose I believe in myself. I believe in the here and now. And in my job. And — " He glanced at Mara. "And I believe in my woman."

"If you believe in your woman, then you must love her," John said.

"Well, I . . . I . . . "

"No need to feel embarrassed," Jesus encouraged. "You should love her. A woman needs love. Every woman does. And especially this woman of yours, Benoni."

Benoni turned to really look at her.

She met his look and held it for a wondrous moment; and while she could not be sure in the softness of the starlight, she thought tiny crystals of tears crept into his eyes.

"And Mara," Jesus said gently, "there is something that all men need. Especially this man of yours."

"And what is that, sir?"

"It is respect. All men need respect. Especially from their women."

"Oh, I respect him, sir. I really do. After all, he is an important man. He is Herod's scribe for this toparchy."

A strange smile crossed Jesus' face.

Mara wondered at its meaning.

"Sometimes, Master," Peter spoke up, "I think that a man must earn such respect."

"No more than a woman should earn love," John said.

Jesus disagreed. "Love and respect are gifts."

"Gifts?" Benoni sounded surprised.

"That's what I found to be so with my wife!" Peter said with a chuckle.

"Peter's wife picks at him sometimes, Benoni," John explained. "When she doesn't is when it's the gift!"

"She dislikes his being away from home so much," James said in a flat, practical way.

"She is well-provided for. She and her mother, too," Peter defended. "I am able to be home enough to provide for them both. Jesus understands about such things."

"James, how did your wife react when you left your fishing business to go with Jesus?" Benoni asked.

"I am not married. Neither is my brother."

"But our father was not happy about our leaving," John inserted. "And each time we return to Capernaum, he argues with Jesus about it."

"Does Jesus ever argue back?"

"Benoni!" Mara admonished, bewildered by such blunt talk in front of the saviour of the world.

Peter, James and John looked at her in surprise.

Benoni shrugged. "His men have spoken bluntly about the problems he has caused by calling them to follow him. And he has not argued back. He speaks of a new kingdom. But the Jews have tried to push out the Romans before, and always have failed. Jesus has only twelve men to help him. How can he possibly bring in a new kingdom? Yet he has not argued back, has not defended his way, nor himself."

"Jesus knows he has no need to argue back," Peter said. "Though we may argue with him, he knows that we are his men, pledged to follow him. We have knowingly pledged this to him. We will continue to follow him. A new kingdom is at hand."

"And you and nine others are going to bring it about?" Benoni's tone was scornful.

John straightened. "Peter is right in what he has said. But there is something more."

"And what is that?"

"We feel free to be honest in front of Jesus. I do admit there are times when we try to hide our true feelings. But somehow, he always knows."

"When we do try to hide our true feelings," James said, "he is distressed by it."

"And in some strange way," John interrupted, "his distress reaches back to touch our own consciences."

"So, in all practicality, it's just easier to be honest in front of him," James finished.

Peter spoke up again. "It is like the bond between a man and woman. Man provides for woman, gives her the gift of love, but in return, he must be able to know that he has the gift of respect from her. He has to be able to trust her. And even to a rough fisherman like me, trust can only be real if it is based on honesty between the man and woman."

An abrupt memory came to Mara of the day Benoni asked her into his house. She stiffened, focusing her mind to recall it fully. But the parts of the memory which jumped at her were Benoni's words, *I need a woman I can trust,* and her own pledge that she was that woman. Now, considering what she was hearing from Jesus and his men, she was reminded once again that she had never told Benoni or anyone else in Sychar that she was married. Once more, she questioned the honesty of her pledge more deeply than ever before.

The fact that Nehushta had so recently found out about Coniah was still an enormous threat, just as it had been before Rakem took her to Jerusalem. If the threat was ever acted on, then her worst fears would become reality. She would have to leave Benoni and return to Coniah. The familiar shroud of rejection and misfortune overtook her once more. She began to tremble.

Jesus noticed and looked at her.

She turned so her face would be hidden from him while her heart cried, *How can I be honest? How can I tell anyone what I have done?*

His spirit heard her silent plea. "Fear not," he said. "The answers to your questions lie within you, Mara. You have but to give them life through honesty."

She would remember his words long afterwards. But for the moment, all she could think of was how hard it would be to tell Benoni she had not been honest with him; and that by not telling him about Coniah, she had placed him in a very dangerous position.

By the time Mara awoke next morning, Jesus and his men had departed from Sychar. But the memory of Jesus' words about trust and honesty were still very much with her.

So was her sense of misfortune and impending doom. She felt like one of the foolish virgins Jesus had spoken of. She rolled over and looked at Benoni still asleep on his own mat. A feeling of remorse went through her.

He had given her a home, food, clothes, friends, and himself. And what had she given him? A lie! A lie about who she really was. But how could she tell him she was a married woman? How could she tell him that now?

She began to rationalize. Maybe she wouldn't have to tell him. Maybe Nehushta's threat was only that, a threat. Maybe Nehushta really had never met Coniah, but had heard his name from her family in Sebaste. Yes, that was most likely what had happened. Nehushta had never really met Coniah, after all. The rationalization made her feel better. She would be a better woman to Benoni than ever before to make up for not telling him about Coniah.

Careful not to awaken him, she rolled up her sleeping mat, stacked it in the far corner of the room, and went out into the courtyard. The heat of the past three days had broken and was replaced by a soft, cooling breeze. Benoni's fine new horse snuffled and turned his head to look at her. She picked up the yoke and leather buckets, and walked toward the well.

Just beyond the city gate, she saw Shua leading the little donkey, Dendo. Two of her friends were with her. Hurrying, she caught up with them. "May the day be blessed for you."

"And for you, Mara."

The other two women nodded and smiled.

"Matri saw our Galilean friends leave Sychar well before the dawn," Shua said. "I wish they could have stayed longer. Jesus could have taught us so much more."

"He taught us a very great deal as it is," Mara replied in a wistful tone.

Shua cast an inquisitive glance at her.

"Was it hard to have the Galileans as your houseguests?" one of the other woman wanted to know.

"It was not hard at all. You and many others in the village were very helpful with your gifts of food. I think it is Shua and Matri who deserve a reward for opening their house to the entire village to hear Jesus preach."

"We were blessed by it. His presence among us was beyond reward," Shua replied.

"I think Mara received a rare blessing," said one of the other women. "For it was she to whom Jesus first proclaimed his messiahship."

A strange mixture of joy and guilt went through Mara. It was a rare blessing to have him speak to her. Joy, unlike any other she had ever known, sprang from that. But later, in his preaching about his new kingdom, and especially in his words to her on the roof, it was as if he held up a mirror that reflected back to her all her own weaknesses and sins. Even more, she was beginning to realize that Jesus expected her to do something about them. They were hers to take care of. Not his.

"Is something wrong, Mara?" Shua asked, looking closely at her.

"Of course not." She slowed her pace and began to fumble with the cords on the buckets to distract Shua's curiosity. She was determined not to reveal any part of the rooftop conversation with Jesus.

Shua slowed her pace, too, waiting for her.

The other two women went on ahead of them.

Mara continued to fumble with the cords, wishing Shua would go on.

But she didn't. She watched Mara for another moment, and then said, "We've all been so busy with Jesus and his men that I forgot to ask Benoni and Rakem if they ever found Nehushta when they were looking for her the other day."

Mara dropped the cords. "What did they want to find her for?"

Shua shook her head. "I thought you might know."

"Well, I don't!" She repositioned the yoke on her shoulders and went forward once again toward the well.

Reaching it, the other women already there greeted them both. Half-heartedly, Mara returned the greetings, in no mood for socializing and village gossip. She was anxious to draw her water and hurry back to ask Benoni about why he had been looking for Nehushta. But the women were slower than usual about drawing their water. They were all talking about Jesus.

"My children had been bothersome, but he made me feel better about them."

"When he spoke of forgiveness, I felt he was talking directly to me."

"He smiled at me and I felt important."

"There was a sense of caring about him."

"I like what he said about honesty and trust. It made me feel closer to my husband."

Mara turned sharply away, pushed her way through the women, and filled her buckets. As she refastened them and slipped the yoke about her shoulders, Jesus' words came back to her. "The answers to your questions lie within you."

Back in the village, Mara set the buckets down in the courtyard, slipped out of the yoke, and without noticing that Benoni's fine new horse was absent, hurried into the house. "Benoni? Are you here?"

A muffled sound came from the inner room.

She went toward it. But as she neared the doorway, a sudden and unexplained fear swept over her. She stopped abruptly and listened. No further sound came from the inner room. She started to call out again, then decided against it. Something inside her told her to run. The thought came too late. Before she could act on it, a man stepped into the room to confront her.

"Coniah!"

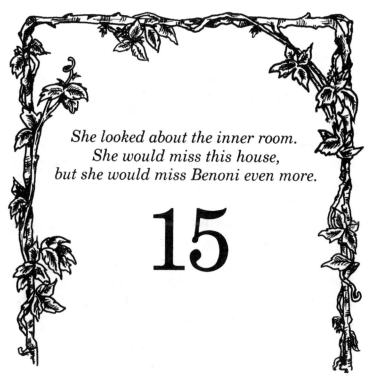

She looked about the inner room.
She would miss this house,
but she would miss Benoni even more.

15

MARA'S HEART went out of her. The thing she had feared the most had happened. Coniah had found her. In spite of all rationalizing, and all prayers, he had found her.

What was worse, she was alone with him. There was no one to help her, to keep him away, to stop him from touching her.

He looked at her with cruel satisfaction. Lust was in his eyes.

A scream started in her throat, but died unfulfilled as the muffled sound from the inner room repeated itself.

Coniah glanced toward the sound.

In that brief instant, she abruptly moved forward, and shoved at him with all her strength.

He stumbled backward, trying to regain his balance, a look of astonishment on his face.

She shoved him again.

He went sprawling backwards, falling, striking his head against Benoni's writing desk. Quills and parchment scrolls flew in all directions, making startled scratch marks of noise.

And then all was quiet, deathly quiet.

Gasping for breath, she stared down at him, not knowing whether he was dead or alive, knowing only that, for the moment, he could not harm her.

The muffled sound came again from the inner room.

She turned and went toward it.

Benoni lay bound and gagged between a basket of corn and a stack of dried papyrus reeds.

She rushed to him, fumbled at the ties that bound him, finally succeeded in freeing him.

"Who is that brute?" he demanded, struggling up onto his feet.

"His name is Coniah," she said, helping him brush the dirt from his robes.

"Coniah? Who is he? What does he want? How do you know him?"

"He is a muleteer from Sebaste."

"A muleteer?" A curious look went across Benoni's face.

She nodded.

"But what does he want here? What caused him to bind me like a sack of corn? What does he want?"

How could she tell him? He would throw her out. He would have to. Custom would demand it. He would throw her out of his house, and out of his life. She could not bear it. Agonizing, she turned from him.

He caught her by both arms, insisting that she face him. "What is it he wants, Mara?"

Her throat went dry.

"Is it you he wants?"

With heaviness in her heart, she nodded.

"Why?"

No words would come.

He shook her. "Why?"

"Because . . . " she said, a sense of shame flaming up inside her. "I am his wife."

He let go of her arms and stood so quietly looking at her that he seemed not even to breathe. There was neither condemnation nor forgiveness in his look. It was impossible to tell what his thoughts really were.

She walked away, knowing that he would want nothing more to do with her. Why should he? He had thought her to be a woman he could trust. And she was not. There was no hope that he could forgive her. Why should he? He was an important man, and she had deliberately concealed from him the truth about herself.

He turned, walked into the main room, and on out into the courtyard.

She looked about the inner room, thinking how much she would miss this house. But she would miss Benoni even more. If only she had been honest with him in the first place, she thought, remembering Jesus' words about respect and love and trust. If she had been honest with Benoni in the first place, she really would have been a woman he could trust. But as it was . . .

She went to the place where she had stored the doll from her childhood. Benoni would expect her to take it. She would take nothing else. No food, not even the new cloak and shawl he had given her. It would be like stealing from him. And she had already stolen enough, she told herself. She had stolen his trust.

From the main room of the house, she heard Coniah stirring. Clutching the doll, she hurried back into the main room just as Benoni came back into the house from the courtyard, carrying the buckets of water she'd left there.

"Get the dipper, Mara," he ordered.

She put down the doll, got the dipper from a small shelf nearby and handed it to him.

He scooped out some of the water from one of the buckets, walked toward the still-groggy Coniah and threw it into his face.

Coniah sputtered, sat up, rubbed at his face, and glared at both of them.

"How much do you want, Coniah?"

"For what?"

"To divorce Mara."

Coniah laughed.

"How much?" Benoni repeated.

"I came to claim her, to take her back."

"Back where?"

"To my house. To Sebaste."

"I don't think you ought to do that."

Coniah tried to get to his feet.

Benoni put his foot on his chest and pushed him back down onto the floor.

Coniah cursed.

"Listen to what I have to say, muleteer. It could save your life."

Coniah cursed again.

"Have you ever been to Caesarea-by-the-Sea?"

"What if I have?"

"And do you sell mules to the Romans?"

"What if I do?"

"Are you ever careless with your mules?"

Coniah narrowed his eyes in a calculating way.

"Have you ever caused accidents to happen because of your carelessness? My Roman friends tell me you have."

"Why should you have Roman friends?"

"All of Herod's scribes have Roman friends."

Surprise crossed Coniah's face.

"Yes, I am one of Herod's scribes. Look about you. You broke my writing desk and you are sitting on a bed of quills and scrolls. You will have to pay me for the damage."

"Pay? Damage? You be damned for that! You stole my wife!" Coniah roared and pushed up onto his feet.

Benoni stood his ground. "Not before you're damned for causing the death of a Roman commander!"

Coniah stopped, stared, took an abrupt step backwards.

Mara felt a ripple of shock. She looked at Benoni, thinking he must be trying to bluff Coniah. But the expression on his face was one of utter seriousness. And then she remembered. Commander Lucius Marcellus, the brother of Tribune Bernardus. Benoni wasn't bluffing. He believed that it was Coniah who had caused the young officer's fatal accident.

"Now I ask you again, Coniah, how much do you want to divorce Mara?"

Coniah glowered at him with such venom that Mara began to tremble. She'd seen the look before. It terrified her. It meant beatings and violence.

In the next instant, Coniah raged forward, hands grasping for Benoni's throat.

With the surprising litheness that belied his weight, Benoni side-stepped, spun around and kicked Coniah in the back.

The larger man stumbled over a small stool, staggered, then grabbed up the stool and hurled it at Benoni.

Again Benoni side-stepped and edged toward the doorway. Coniah pulled a small dagger from his waistband and moved toward him, menacing, demanding satisfaction.

Mara screamed, rushed forward, flung herself at Coniah's back and grasped frantically for the dagger in his upraised hand.

The action completely surprised Coniah. In the instant it took him to react to it, Benoni attacked him from the front and wrestled the dagger from his grasp.

"I should kill you!" Benoni threatened, holding the dagger near Coniah's throat.

The big man's eyes bulged with terror.

"No, Benoni," Mara cried out. "You must not kill him."

"I have every right to kill him."

"No, Benoni. No!"

"Why not kill him? It would solve every problem. Why not kill him?"

"Because it is wrong."

"By whose word?"

"By the Nazarene's word."

The response came spontaneously and uncalled. It surprised her as much as it surprised Benoni.

He glanced at her in astonishment.

"And by the commandments which God gave to Moses. 'Thou shalt not kill.' "

"I know nothing of your Moses, and less about your god."

"But you know Jesus," she said with gentle firmness. "And here, in this house, he taught us to love our neighbors."

The expression on Benoni's face altered.

"No matter how often I might have wished Coniah dead, I could not stand it if you or I were the ones to kill him."

"Next, you'll want to *forgive* this hulking frame of violence!"

She straightened. The idea of forgiveness had never before crossed her mind where Coniah was concerned. And though she knew Benoni meant it in a different way, she was instantly reminded of the importance that Jesus had placed on forgiveness. "Why not?" she said. "Why not forgive Coniah?"

The expression on Benoni's face altered again.

"Why should we have Coniah on our consciences?" she said in a matter-of-fact tone that belied the funny tug taking place in her heart. "Why indeed?"

For the third time, Benoni's expression changed, this time reflecting how seriously he was considering the logic of her words.

Benoni slowly relaxed his grip on Coniah, but continued to hold the dagger near his throat. "Again I ask you to divorce Mara. Say that is what you will do and I will write a paper for you to mark. It will set you free and it will set her free. It is man's law to do it that way."

The sounds of the skirmish had escaped the walls of the house and spilled into the streets. Villagers were running from all directions. Some were curious. Some were concerned. Some even wanted to help. Rakem was among the first to arrive.

"What's your answer, muleteer?" Benoni insisted. "Do you agree to divorce her? Or do I turn you over to the Romans?"

Coniah shook free. "I divorce her. Here and now."

Benoni handed the dagger to Rakem. "Watch him."

Mara crossed the room, propped up the writing desk as best she could, searched through the scattered quills for an unbroken one, and prepared a small amount of charcoal and water for Benoni to use.

Benoni took only a short time to write the document and put his official seal on it. "Hear what I have written," he said, turning back to Coniah. "'I do hereby put away from me Mara of Sychar. I no longer consider her my property. She is no longer my wife.'"

Rakem glanced questioningly at Mara.

Benoni shoved a quill into Coniah's hand. "Make your mark on it!"

The muleteer made a mark. "Good riddance. The woman was used merchandise from the beginning."

Mara blushed.

"The Romans will think less than that of you," Benoni said, getting up from the writing desk. "Once they catch you, they will crucify you for the death of that young commander."

Coniah's head jerked around. Fresh terror bulged in his eyes.

"And catch you, they will," Benoni continued. "And crucify you, they will."

Coniah spat at Benoni, shoved Rakem aside, and raced for the inner room of the house and its hidden doorway to freedom.

Mara tried to stop him.

"Let him go," Benoni ordered.

"Let him go?"

"I'll send word to Tribune Bernardus about who he is and where to find him. We'll see no more of him here in Sychar."

"Nor of Nehusta, either, if my guess is right," Rakem said, brushing at his robes.

"Coniah and Nehusta deserve each other," Benoni said with a grim laugh.

Rakem went out into the courtyard to reassure the villagers that all was well within, that the danger had passed and that they could all return to their houses.

Mara sank down on the doorstep, shocked by all that had happened so quickly, and grateful that it was over. She glanced skyward. Clouds moved aimlessly across the great blue dome, building and eroding patterns of light and shadow before her very eyes. They drifted without seeming purpose, much like her life always had.

Once, she would not have questioned whether her life should even have a purpose. Now, if she believed anything at all that Jesus had said, her life did have purpose. So did Benoni's. She would have to tell him about her other husbands. She must be honest with him, and now she knew she could be. And he—? Well, he would have to stop forging documents, and he could no longer charge people extra for reading and writing for them, and he would have to marry her, even though now she would be in every way a woman he could trust.

He came and sat down on the doorstep beside her. In his hands he held her treasured childhood doll. "You are a courageous woman, even though a prisoner of fear."

"I think meeting Jesus must have changed me."

"Meeting him has changed me, too."

She smiled at him.

"I think we should tell others about him," Benoni said.

"You do, really?"

He nodded. "You are the first person to be told that he is the Messiah. I believe you are meant to share that knowledge. And I want to help."

"I knew you liked Jesus. But I didn't know you believed in him."

He handed the doll to her, put his arm around her protectively, and pulled her close. "It's not hard to believe in him once you have met him."

A feeling of joy coursed through her. The old feelings of doom and misfortune were gone. This time she felt they would not return. In fact, she knew it in her bones.

Quality Christian Fiction
from Here's Life Publishers

Biblical Fiction by Gloria Howe Bremkamp

A Woman Called Magdalene (July '91)

Phoebe: A Leader Before Her Time (March '92)

The Nicki Holland Mysteries—a bright new series for junior-age girls from award-winning author Angela Elwell Hunt

The Case of the Mystery Mark (May '91)

The Case of the Phantom Friend (May '91)

The Case of the Teenage Terminator (May '91)

At Christian bookstores everywhere.

Or call

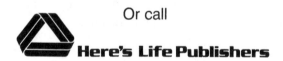

Here's Life Publishers

1-800-950-4457

(Visa and Mastercard accepted)

MAR 304-9